Dear Reader,

Looking back over the years, I find it hard to realise that twenty-six of them have gone by since I wrote my first book—*Sister Peters in Amsterdam*. It wasn't until I started writing about her that I found that once I had started writing, nothing was going to make me stop—and at that time I had no intention of sending it to a publisher. It was my daughter who urged me to try my luck.

I shall never forget the thrill of having my first book accepted. A thrill I still get each time a new story is accepted. Writing to me is such a pleasure, and seeing a story unfolding on my old typewriter is like watching a film and wondering how it will end. Happily of course.

To have so many of my books re-published is such a delightful thing to happen and I can only hope that those who read them will share my pleasure in seeing them on the bookshelves again. . .and enjoy reading them.

Back by Popular Demand

A collector's edition of favourite titles from one of the world's best-loved romance authors. Mills & Boon are proud to bring back these sought after titles and present them as one cherished collection.

BETTY NEELS: COLLECTOR'S EDITION

TEMPESTUOUS APRIL

BY
BETTY NEELS

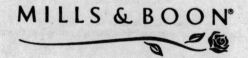

MILLS & BOON and MILLS & BOON with the Rose Device are registered trademarks of the publisher.

First published in Great Britain 1970 by Mills & Boon Limited
This edition 1998
Harlequin Mills & Boon Limited,
Eton House, 18-24 Paradise Road, Richmond, Surrey TW9 1SR

© Betty Neels 1970

ISBN 0 263 80669 3

Set in Times Roman 11 on 12½ pt by
Rowland Phototypesetting Limited
Bury St Edmunds, Suffolk

73-9804-46171

Made and printed in Great Britain by
Caledonian International Book Manufacturing Ltd, Glasgow

CHAPTER ONE

MEN'S Surgical was quiet—there had been two emergency admissions before midnight; a case in theatre—a rather nasty appendix—at one o'clock, and a cardiac arrest at half past two; these happenings interspersed by old Mr Gadd's frequent and successful attempts to climb over his cot sides and amble down the ward in search of refreshment. But none of these happenings appeared to have upset Miss Harriet Slocombe, sitting, as neat as a new pin, at Sister's desk, writing the bare bones of her report. She appeared to be as fresh as the proverbial daisy and would have been genuinely surprised if anyone had suggested to her that she had had a busy night. She sucked the top of her ballpoint and frowned at the clatter of plates from the kitchen where her junior nurse was cutting bread and butter for the patients' breakfasts. It was four o'clock, almost time for her, in company with Nurse Potter, to consume the tea and toast with which they fortified themselves before beginning their early morning work. Miss Slocombe removed the pen from her mouth and got up in order to do a round of her patients. She went

from bed to bed, making no sound, due very
largely to the fact that she had removed her shoes
from her feet some time previously, and was in
her stockings. The shoes stood side by side under
Sister's desk, waiting to be donned again after
her tea break. She reached the end of the ward
and paused by the windows opening on to the
balcony, to look out into the chill gloom of the
early morning. March could be dreary; especially just before dawn. She stood watching the
fine drizzle and thought with pleasure of the
three-week holiday she was to have in a fort-
night's time. . .and at the end of it she would be
coming back to St Nick's as Ward Sister of
Men's Surgical. A rosy future, she told herself
robustly, and sighed. She was twenty-four years
old and pretty, with wide blue eyes, a retroussé
nose and a gently curving mouth; she wore her
bright blonde hair—the envy of her friends—in
a complicated knot on top of her head, and her
person was small, so that she looked extremely
fragile. She was in fact, as strong as an ox. She
had a faint air of reserve and a nasty temper
when roused, which was seldom. She was liked
by everyone in the hospital with the possible
exception of one or two of the housemen, who
had expected her to be as fragile as her appearance and were still smarting from her astringent
tongue. They called her Haughty Harry amongst
themselves, and when she had heard about it,

she had laughed with everybody else, but a little wistfully, because she knew that with the right man she wouldn't be in the least haughty. . . She sighed again, and went to tuck up Mr Gadd who had, as usual, fallen sound asleep at the wrong end of the night. In the next bed to him, the theatre case opened hazy eyes and said in a woolly drugged voice,

'Cor, dang me, you'm as pretty as a picture,' and went immediately to sleep again.

Harriet smiled, a warm, motherly smile, wholly without conceit; she was aware that she was a pretty girl, but two elder sisters and three brothers younger than herself had taught her at an early age to put things in their proper perspective. She had long since outgrown her youthful dreams of captivating some young, handsome and wealthy man with her good looks; but outgrown though they might be, they had so far made it impossible for her to settle for anything less. She moved soundlessly down the ward, adjusted two drips, took a blood pressure and carefully and gently examined the two emergencies; they were sleeping soundly. She supposed that they would go to Theatre during the day. She reached the last bed and stood a moment facing the quiet ward, listening. She ignored the snores, the sighs and Mr Bolt's tracheostomy tube's faint whistle, she ignored the background sissing of the hot water pipes and the soft rhythm of the electric pump beneath young Butcher's bed—all these sounds were familiar; she knew who and what made them. It was other sounds she was listening for—a change in breathing, an unexpectedly sudden restlessness and more sinister—the quiet from a bed where there should be the small sounds of a sleeping man. Her trained ear detected nothing untoward, however, and she nodded, well satisfied, and turned to Sister's table, just as Nurse Potter, plump and beaming, edged herself round the ward door with a tray. She put it down carefully and whispered breathily,

'I made Bovril toast, Staff,' and indicated the generous pile before them. Harriet was already pouring out the tea.

'Good. I love it and I'm famished. I only hope we'll get the chance to eat it all.'

They began to munch, and presently, when their hunger was a little blunted, Harriet started to plan the morning's work.

Night nurses' breakfast was always a noisy meal—everyone talked and laughed with a false energy inspired by the knowledge that the night was over once more. The paralysis of tiredness which had crept over them in the early hours of the morning had been forgotten. Later, it would return, so that those who weren't already in bed were liable to sleep in the bath or drop off over a late morning cup of cocoa—in the meantime they were all bursting with vigour. The staff nurses sat at a table on their own; there were perhaps a dozen of them, of whom Harriet was the last to arrive that morning. Late though she was, she looked unruffled and incredibly neat and not in the least tired.

'We stayed to help,' she volunteered as she sat down. 'There's been an accident at the brickworks.'

There was an understanding murmur—the brickworks was notorious for the fact that it could always be relied upon to fill any vacant bed in Men's Surgical at all times.

She was left to to make a substantial breakfast at her leisure, and not until she had poured her third cup of tea did someone ask,

'Has anyone seen the new RMO? I ought to have done—after all, I am on Medical, but all I got last night was our Mr Rugg.' Mr Rugg was young and uncertain and definitely not a lady's man. The speaker looked around the table until her eye lighted upon Harriet, who had gone a delicious pink.

'I might have known. . . Harry, where did you meet him?'

Harry put down her cup. 'He came on to the ward last night,' she said serenely. 'We had that cardiac arrest, remember?' She looked inside the empty teapot and put it down again resignedly. 'He's nice—good-looking and one of those gravelly voices and polished manners—' She was interrupted by a chorus of knowing groans; when they had subsided she added gently, 'He's engaged.'

A disappointed voice asked, 'How do you know? He couldn't have had time to tell you that!'

'He talked while he was making up the chart. I expect he felt lonely and wanted to talk about her. Perhaps I've got a sympathetic face,' she observed hopefully, and was greeted by a shriek of friendly laughter; her friends and acquaintances holding the opinion that anyone as pretty as Harry Slocombe needed to be nothing else. After a moment she laughed with them, privately wondering why everyone other than her own family attached such importance to looks.

A couple of hours later she was sitting up in bed reading sleepily when there was a knock on the door and a tall well-built girl came in.

Harriet put her book down. 'Sieske, you're never on at eleven again?'

The girl nodded gloomily and came to sit on the end of the bed. She was nice-looking, with a pleasant, placid face framed in pale hair which she wore in an unfashionable and highly becoming bun in the nape of her neck.

'Aunt Agnes must loathe me,' she remarked. Aunt Agnes was the Sister on Men's Medical, she had been there for unnumbered years and made a habit of loathing everyone. 'It is because I am not English, you think?'

Harriet shook her head. 'She never likes anyone. I shouldn't worry anyway, it's only another two weeks, isn't it? I shall miss you, Sieske.'

'Me you too,' said Sieske with obscure sincerity. She patted her bun with a large capable and very beautiful hand and turned solemn blue eyes on Harriet.

'Harry, will you not come with me when I go? You have three weeks' holiday; you could see much of Holland in that time—we should all be so glad; my family think of you as a friend, you know. I tell them many times of my visits to your home—we shall be highly pleased to have you as guest. It is a quiet place where we live, but we have many friends, and the country is pretty too.' She paused and went on shyly, 'I should like you to meet Wierd.' Wierd was her fiancé; after several months of friendship with Sieske, Harriet looked upon him as an old friend, just as the Dutch girl's family—her mother and father, younger sisters and the older brother who had just qualified as a doctor at Leiden—seemed like old friends too. The Dutch girl had told her so much about them that she felt that she already knew them. It would be delightful to go and stay with Sieske and meet them all—there was a partner too, she remembered; mentioned casually from time to time. Harriet searched her sleep-clogged brain for his name. Friso Eijsinck. She didn't know much more about him than his name, though. Sieske had mentioned too that he wasn't married. Harriet felt faintly sympathetic towards him, picturing him as a middle-aged bachelor with a soup-stained waistcoat. She dismissed his vague image from her mind.

'I'd love to come,' she said warmly. 'But are you sure it will be all right with your family?'

Sieske smiled. 'But of course I am sure. Already they have written with an invitation, which I extend to you. I am most happy, as they will be. We will make plans together for the journey.' She got up. 'Now you will sleep and I will write to Moeder.'

'We'll arrange it all on my nights off,' said Harriet sleepily. 'Get a day off and come home with me—tell Aunt Agnes you have to go to your grandmother's funeral.'

'A joke?' queried Sieske. She had a hand on the door but paused to look back doubtfully at Harriet. But Harriet was already asleep.

Harriet's family lived in a small west country village some forty miles from the city where she worked. Her father had had a practice there for twenty-five years or more and lived in a roomy rather ramshackle house that had sheltered his large family with ease, and now housed a growing band of grandchildren during school holidays. His eldest son had just qualified in his turn and had already taken his place in the wide-flung practice. It was he who fetched the two girls from hospital a few days later. He owned an elderly Sprite, which was always over-loaded with passengers, but both girls were used to travelling in this cramped fashion and packed themselves in without demur. The country looked fresh and green after the rain, the moors rolled away into the distance—Harriet tied a scarf tightly round her hair and drew a deep breath; she was always happiest where the horizon was wide. The village looked cosy, with its thatched and cob walled cottages; the daffodils were out in the doctor's garden as they shot up the drive and stopped with a tooth-jolting jerk at the front door. The girls scrambled out and ran inside to the comfort of the shabby hall and thence to the big sitting-room at the back of the house, where Mrs Slocombe was waiting with tea and the warm welcome she offered to anyone who set foot inside her home. She listened to the girls' plans as they ate their way through home-made scones with a great deal of butter and jam, and the large fruit cake Mrs Slocombe had thoughtfully baked against their coming. She refilled their cups and said calmly, 'How lovely for you, Harry darling. You'll need a passport and a photo—better go into town tomorrow and get them settled. How will you go?'

Sieske answered, 'From Harwich. We can go by train from the Hoek and my father will meet us at Leeuwarden.'

Mrs Slocombe replenished the teapot. 'Travel broadens the mind,' she observed, and looked at Harriet, immersed in a map. Such a dear child, and so unlike her brothers and sisters with her delicate prettiness and femininity and so gently pliant until one encountered the sturdy core of proud independence and plain common sense beneath it. Mrs Slocombe sighed. It would be nice to see Harriet happily married as her two sisters were. Heaven knew it wasn't for lack of opportunity, the dear girl was surrounded by men as though they were bees round a honeypot; and she treated all of them as though they were brothers. Perhaps she would meet some nice man in Holland. Mrs Slocombe smiled happily at the thought and gave her mind to the serious business of the right clothes to take.

They spent the rest of that evening making their plans, helped and sometimes hindered by the advice and suggestions proffered by members of the family and their friends as they drifted in and out of the sitting-room. Her brother William, coming in from evening surgery, remarked with all the experience of someone who had been to the Continent of Europe on several occasions, 'Still at it? Good lord, Harry, anyone would think you were going to the other side of the world instead of the other side of the North Sea.'

His sister remained unmoved by his observations, and merely picked up a small cushion and threw it at his head with the unerring aim of much practice. 'Beast,' she said affectionately. 'But it is the other side of the world to me, isn't it? I've never been outside Britain before, so any part of the world is foreign—just as foreign as the other side of the world—and everyone I meet will be a foreigner.'

This ingenuous remark caused a great deal of merriment. 'I hope,' said William, half seriously, 'that you'll remember that you are going to be the foreigner.'

'Harriet will not feel foreign with us,' said Sieske stoutly. 'We all speak English—that is, Father and Aede and Friso speak it very well, and Maggina and Taeike are learning it at school—only my mother does not speak it though she does at times understand.'

'And then there's you,' pointed out Harriet. 'You speak marvellous English.'

Sieske glowed with pleasure. 'Yes, I think I do, but then you helped me very much; it is not an easy language to learn.'

'Nor, I gather, is Dutch,' remarked Dr Slocombe dryly, 'although it doesn't sound as though Harry will need to know one word of it.'

'No, of course she won't,' agreed Mrs

Slocombe comfortably. She looked across the room at her daughter and thought with maternal satisfaction what a very pretty girl she was. A great deal could happen in three weeks, whatever part of the world one happened to be in.

CHAPTER TWO

THEY travelled by the night boat from Harwich, and Harriet, whose longest sea trip had been between Penzance and the Scillies, was disagreeably surprised to find the North Sea so spiteful. She lay in her bunk, listening to Sieske's gentle breathing above her, and wondered if she would be seasick. It was fortunate that she fell asleep while she was still making up her mind about this, and didn't wake up until the stewardess wakened them with their early morning tea. It was delightful to take turns with Sieske, to peer out of the porthole at the low coast of Holland. It looked as flat as she had always imagined it would be, and lonely as well. An hour later, however, disembarking amidst the cheerful bustle, she reversed her opinion. There seemed to be a great many people, all working very hard and apparently delighted to see the passengers coming off the boat; a larger porter took their luggage and led them to the Customs shed, exchanging pleasantries with Sieske, and thumped down their cases in front of a small rat-faced man who asked them in a surprisingly pleasant voice why they had come and what they had brought with them. Here again Sieske was useful; Harriet found that she did not need to utter a word, although she said 'Thank you' politely when she was handed her passport, and was taken aback when the Customs Officer wished her a happy holiday—in quite beautiful English.

The train snaked silently through green meadows where black and white cows, coated against the chilly wind, stood placidly to watch them flash by; there were farms dotted here and there, with steep roofs, and gardens arranged very neatly around them—the villages were dominated by their churches; Harriet had never seen so many soaring steeples in her life, nor, for that matter, had she seen so many factories, each with its small satellite of new houses close by. She didn't like them very much and turned with relief to the contemplation of a canal, running like a ruler through the neat countryside, and carrying a variety of picturesque traffic. Presently they were served coffee and ham rolls, and the two girls sat back, watching the country flash by under a blue, rather watery sky stretching away to the flat horizon. In no time at all they were at Rotterdam—Harriet watched the early morning crowds racing to work with a faintly smug sympathy. The three weeks of her holiday stretching ahead of her seemed a very long time indeed. She wondered idly what she would feel like on the return journey. Once they had left Rotterdam, the scenery became more rural, the villages lying neatly amongst the flat meadows, like cakes arranged tidily on a plate—Gouda, even from a distance, looked intriguing—Harriet wished that they might have stopped to look around, but the train went remorselessly on to Utrecht and then to Amersfoort, where they had to get out anyway and change trains. They stood on the platform and watched the express rush away towards the frontier, and then because they had half an hour to wait, they went and had a cup of coffee and Sieske spread the incredibly small Dutch money on the table between them and gave Harriet her first lesson. They laughed a great deal and the time passed so quickly that they were surprised when the train for Leeuwarden arrived and they were stowed on board by a kindly porter, who tossed their cases in after them and waved cheerfully as the train pulled out.

They still had a two-hour journey before them, Harriet settled herself by the window once more, listening to Sieske's unhurried voice and watching the subtle changing of the countryside. It began to look very like the New Forest, with stretches of heath and charming little woods; there were glimpses of houses too, not large, but having an air of luxury, each set in its own immaculate grounds. Presently the woods and

heathland gave way in their turn to rolling grass-
land. The farms looked large and prosperous,
even the cows looked plumply outsize and
although there were plenty of villages and towns
there was a refreshing lack of factories.

Sieske's father was waiting at Leeuwarden, a
large, very tall man with thick grey hair, a neat
moustache and an elegant Van Dyke beard. He
had a round merry face, but his eyes were shrewd
behind the horn-rimmed glasses he wore. He
greeted Sieske with a bear-like hug and a flow
of incomprehensible words, but as he turned to
shake Harriet's hand, she was relieved to find
that his English was almost as good as her own.

'You are most welcome, Harriet,' he said
warmly. 'We hope that you will have a pleasant
holiday with us—and now we will go home;
Mother is waiting—she is most excited, but she
would not come with me because everything has
to be ready for you when you arrive.'

He led the way over to a BMW, and Harriet
looked at it with an appreciative eye as they got
in. She gazed around her as they went through
Leeuwarden, glimpsing small side streets that
would be fun to explore. Dr Van Minnen seemed
to read her thoughts, for without taking his eyes
off the road, he said, 'You shall come here,
Harriet, and look around one day soon. There is
a great deal to see as well as a museum of which
we are very proud.'

Franeker, Sieske's home, was only a short distance from Leeuwarden; in less than twenty minutes they were slowing down past a large church and turning into the main street of the charming little town.

The doctor lived in a large house overlooking a tree-lined canal which ran between narrow cobbled streets lined with buildings from another era. No two houses were alike, except in a shared dignity of age and beauty. Harriet got out of the car and stood gaping at the variety of rooftops. She would have liked to have asked about them, but Sieske was already at the great wooden door with its imposing fanlight, and the doctor caught hold of her arm and hurried her inside behind his daughter, to be greeted by his wife. Mevrouw Van Minnen was very like her daughter and still remarkably youthful—there was no hint of grey in her pale blonde hair and her eyes were as bright a blue as Sieske's; she was a big woman, but there was nothing middle-aged in her brisk movements. The next hour or so was taken up most agreeably, drinking coffee and eating the crisp little biscuits—*sprits*—that went with it. There was a great deal of conversation which lost none of its zest by reason of Harriet's lack of Dutch, and Mevrouw Van Minnen's scant knowledge of English. Presently they all went upstairs to show Harriet her room—it overlooked the street, so that she could see the canal below, which delighted her; and although it was small it was very comfortable. She unpacked happily; it was, she decided, going to be a delightful holiday. She did her hair and her face and went downstairs to join the family for *koffie-tafel*, and ate her bread and cold meat and cheese and omelette with a healthy appetite which called forth delighted surprise from Mevrouw Van Minnen, who had thought she had looked too delicate to do more than peck at her food. Sieske translated this to Harriet, giggling a great deal, and then said in Dutch to her mother:

'Harry isn't quite what she looks, Moeder. She appears to be a fairy, but she's not in the least delicate; and of course it notices here, doesn't it, because we're all so big.'

'Such a pretty girl, too,' her mother murmured. 'I wonder what Aede and Friso will say when they see her.'

Aede wouldn't be home until the evening, it seemed, and no one knew what Friso was doing—he had taken the morning surgery so that Dr Van Minnen could go to Leeuwarden—he had presumably gone to his own home. They would see him later, said Mevrouw Van Minnen comfortably, and suggested that the two girls went out for a walk so that Harriet could see something of the town.

An hour later, the two of them were strolling along looking in the shop windows while Sieske carefully explained the prices. They had reached a particularly interesting display of clocks and jewellery when Sieske suddenly exclaimed, 'I forgot, I have to buy stamps for Father—the post office is in the next street. Wait here, Harry—you can practise your Dutch in this window—I won't be a minute.'

Harriet looked her fill, and then because Sieske still hadn't come back, went to the edge of the pavement and looked up and down the street. It was surprisingly busy for a small town, with a constant thin stream of traffic. She was standing on the corner outside the beautiful town hall and she watched idly as the various buses and lorries halted by her; the cars were mostly small, so that when an AC 428 Fastback pulled up it caught her attention immediately. There was a girl sitting in the front by the driver—a girl so dark that it was impossible not to notice her amongst the fair-haired giants around the town, thought Harriet; she was quite beautiful too. She turned her head and stared at Harriet with great black eyes which barely noticed her. She looked cross, and Harriet, with that extraordinary feeling that in someone else's country you can do things you wouldn't do in your own, stared back openly before transferring her gaze to the driver. He was looking ahead and she studied his profile at her leisure; it was a handsome one, with a domineering nose and a firm chin; his forehead was high and wide and his very fair hair was brushed smoothly back from it. Looking at him, she had the sudden deep conviction that they had met before; her heart started to race, she wished with all her heart that he would turn and look at her. As though she had shouted her wish out loud at him, he turned his head and she found herself gazing into level grey eyes. It seemed to her that she had known him—a complete stranger—all her life; she smiled with the sudden delight of it, wondering if he felt the same way too. Apparently he did not; there was no expression on his face at all, and she went slowly pink under his cool stare. The traffic ahead of him sorted itself out, and he was gone, leaving her gazing sadly after him; the man who had been in her thoughts for so many years; the reason for her being more than friends with the men she had met. He had been her dream; but dreams didn't last. A good thing perhaps, as quite obviously she had no part in his; indeed, he had looked at her as though she had been a lamp-post.

Sieske came back then, and said, 'Harry, what is it? You look as though you've seen a ghost.'

Harriet turned to walk beside her friend. 'No, not a ghost.' She so obviously didn't want to say any more that Sieske bit off the questions she was going to ask, and started to talk about something quite different.

Aede arrived after tea—which wasn't a meal at all, Harriet discovered, just a cup of tea with no milk and a plate of delicate little biscuits. He was like his father, tall and broad, and looked younger than his twenty-five years. He had just qualified as a doctor and was at the hospital at Leeuwarden working as a houseman, and it would be at least another six months before he started to specialize; eventually, of course, he would join his father's practice. He told Harriet these interesting facts in fluent English, sitting beside her on the comfortable sofa near the stove. He drank the decidedly cool tea without apparently minding in the least, and consumed the remainder of the biscuits. Harriet liked him; he wasn't as placid as Sieske, but he was obviously good-natured and an excellent companion. They sat around happily talking shop until almost supper time, while Mevrouw Van Minnen, looking almost as young as her daughter, sat in a straight-backed chair by her work table, knitting a sock at speed and managing to take a lion's share in the talk despite the fact that everything had to be said twice in both languages.

They sat down to the evening meal soon after seven, with a great deal of laughing and talking. Dr Van Minnen, who had disappeared soon after tea to take his evening surgery, came back in time to dispense an excellent sherry from a beautiful decanter into crystal glasses.

'Where's Friso?' inquired his wife. 'He hasn't called to see Sieske.'

The doctor answered her and then repeated his words, this time in English for Harriet's benefit. 'My partner has had to go to Dongjum, a small village a few miles from this town—an extended breech, so he's likely to be there most of the night.'

Harriet felt a pang of pity for the poor man— she had been told that he didn't live in Franeker, but in a nearby village close to the sea; he looked after the rural side of the practice while Dr Van Minnen attended his patients in Franeker.

'Is Dr Eijsinck's share of the practice a large one?' she asked Aede.

'*Hemel*, yes—and very scattered, but he's a glutton for work.'

And Harriet added a harassed expression and a permanent stoop to the stained waistcoat, and then forgot all about him in the excitement of discussing Sieske's and Wierd's engagement party, when their forthcoming marriage would be announced. It was to be a splendid affair, with the *burgemeester* and the *dominee* and various colleagues of the doctor coming, as well as a great many young people. It was fortunate that the sitting-room and the drawing-room were connected by folding doors, which could be pushed back, making one room. Harriet sat back, listening quietly and wondering which of her two party dresses she had had the forethought to bring with her she should wear. Every now and then she thought about the man in the AC 428 Fastback.

The following morning after breakfast, Harriet took the post along to the doctor in his surgery. She hadn't been there yet, but she had been told the way. She went down the long narrow passage leading to the back of the house and through the little door in the wall opposite the kitchen. She could hear a murmur of sound—shuffling feet, coughs and a baby crying, as she knocked on the surgery door. The doctor was alone, searching through a filing cabinet with concentrated fierceness. His voice was mild enough, however, as he remarked.

'Mevrouw Van Hoeve's card is here somewhere—the poor woman is in the waiting room, but how can I give her an injection until I check her notes?'

Harriet put the post down on the desk. It seemed that doctors were all the same the world over.

'I've brought your post,' she said soothingly. 'If you'll spell the name to me I'll look for the card while you see if there's anything important. . .'

Dr Van Minnen gave her a grateful look. 'I

do have an assistant,' he explained, 'but she's on holiday.'

He sat down with a relieved sigh and picked up the first of his letters, and Harriet started to go through the filing cabinet. Mevrouw Van Hoeve was half-way through the second drawer, filed away under P-S; no wonder she couldn't be found. Harriet took it out and turned round in triumph to find that the door had opened and a man had come in; he spoke briefly to Dr Van Minnen and stood staring at her with the same cool grey eyes that she had been trying so hard to forget. She stood staring back at him in her turn, clutching the folder to her; her pretty mouth agape, while the bright colour flooded her face.

Dr Van Minnen glanced up briefly from his desk. 'Harriet, this is my partner, Friso Eijsinck.'

The Friso she had imagined disintegrated. This elegant waistcoat had never borne a soup stain in its well-cared-for life; indeed, the whole appearance of its wearer was one of a well-dressed man about town. There was no sign of a stoop either; he was a giant among the giantlike people around her and he wore his great height with a careless arrogance; and as for the harassed expression—she tried her best to imagine him presenting anything but a calm, controlled face to the world, and failed utterly.

She said, 'How do you do, Doctor,' in a voice which would have done credit to one of Miss

Austen's young ladies, and this time she didn't smile.

His own, 'How do you do, Miss Slocombe,' was uttered in a deep, rather slow voice with a faint impatience in its tones. There was a pause, during which she realized that he was waiting for her to go. She closed the filing cabinet carefully, smiled at Dr Van Minnen, and walked without haste to the door which he was holding open for her, and passed him with no more than a brief glance, her head very high. To her chagrin he wasn't even looking at her. Outside, with the door closed gently behind her, she stopped and reviewed the brief, disappointing meeting. She doubted if he had looked at her—not to see her, at any rate; he had made her feel in the way, and awkward, and this without saying anything at all. She walked on slowly; perhaps he hated the English, or, she amended honestly, he didn't like her.

Sieske was calling her from the top of the house and she went upstairs and put on her clove pink raincoat and tugged its matching hat on to her bright hair, then went shopping with Sieske and her mother.

Wierd was coming that evening. Harriet spent the afternoon setting Sieske's hair, and after their tea combed it out and arranged it for her, then stood back to admire her handiwork. What with a pretty hair-do and the prospect of seeing Wierd

again, Sieske looked like a large and a very
good-looking angel.

There was no evening surgery that day; they
were to meet in the drawing-room for drinks at
six-thirty. Harriet went upstairs to change her
dress wondering what she was going to do until
that time. She suspected that the arrangement
had been made so that Sieske and her young
man would have some time to themselves before
the family assembled. She was just putting the
last pin into her hair when there was a knock
on the door, and when she called 'Come in',
Aede put his inquiring head into the room.

'Harriet? Are you ready? I wondered if you
would like to put on a coat and come for a quick
run in the car—there's heaps of time.'

She had already caught up the pink raincoat;
it wasn't raining any more, but it lay handy on
a chair and she put it on, saying,

'I'd love to, Aede. But do we tell someone?'

They were going downstairs. 'I told Moeder,'
he said. 'She thought it was a jolly good idea.'

His car was outside—a Volkswagen and
rather battered. Harriet got in, remarking knowledgeably that it was a good car and how long
had he had it. This remark triggered off a conversation which lasted them out of Franeker and
several miles along the main road. When he
turned off, however, she asked, 'Where are
we going?'

'Just round the country so that you can see what it is like,' Aede replied, and turned the car into a still smaller road. The country looked green and pleasant in the spring evening light. The farms stood well apart from each other, each joined to its own huge barn by a narrow corridor at its back. They looked secure and prosperous and very different from the more picturesque, less compact English farms. They passed through several small villages with unpronounceable names in the Fries language, then circled back and crossed the main road again so that they were going towards the coast. On the outskirts of one village there was a large house, with an important front door and neat windows across its face. It had a curved gabled roof and a large garden alive with daffodils and tulips and hyacinths. Harriet cried out in delight, 'Oh, Aede, stop—please stop! I simply must stare. Will anyone mind?'

He pulled up obligingly and grinned. 'No, of course not. It is rather lovely, isn't it?'

'And the house,' she breathed, 'that's lovely too. How old is it? Who lives there?'

'About 1760, I think, but you can ask Friso next time you see him; it's his.'

Harriet turned an astonished face to her companion. 'You mean Dr Eijsinck? He lives there? All by himself?'

Aede started the car again. He nodded. 'Yes,

that is, if you don't count a gardener and a cook and a valet and a housemaid or two. He's got a great deal of money, you know; he doesn't need to be a doctor, but his work is the love of his life. That doesn't mean to say that he doesn't love girls too,' he added on a laugh.

'Why doesn't he marry, then?' She waited for Aede's answer. Perhaps Friso was engaged or at least in love; what about that dark girl in his car?

Aede thought for a moment. 'I don't know,' he said slowly. 'I asked him once—oh, a long time ago, and he said he was waiting for the girl.' He shrugged his wide shoulders. 'It didn't make much sense. . .' He broke off. 'Here's Franeker again; we're a bit late, but I don't suppose it will matter.'

Harriet smiled at him. 'It was lovely, Aede. I enjoyed every minute of it.'

He brought the car to a rather abrupt halt in front of the house and they both went inside.

'I'll be down in a minute,' said Harriet, and flew upstairs, to throw down her raincoat, look hastily at herself in the mirror and then race downstairs again. Almost at the bottom of the staircase she checked herself abruptly and continued down to the hall with steps as sedate as the voice with which she greeted Dr Eijsinck, whom she had observed at that very moment standing there. Disconcertingly he didn't answer, and she stood looking up at him——he was in her way, but his size precluded her from passing him unless she pushed by. It seemed a long time before he said reluctantly,

'You smiled. Why?' He gave her a hard, not too friendly stare. 'You didn't know me.'

So he had seen her after all. Harriet felt her heart thudding and ignored it. She said in a steady voice,

'No, I didn't know who you were, Dr Eijsinck. It was just. . .I thought that I recognized you.' Which was, she thought, perfectly true, although she could hardly explain to him that she had dreamed about him so often that she couldn't help but recognize him.

He nodded, and said, to surprise her, 'Yes, I thought perhaps it was that. It happens to us all, I suppose, that once or twice in a lifetime we meet someone who should be a stranger, and is not.'

She longed to ask him what he meant and dared not, and instead said in a stiff, conversational voice,

'What excellent English you speak, Doctor,' and came to a halt at the amused look on his face. And there was amusement in his voice when he answered.

'How very kind of you to say so, Miss Slocombe.'

She looked down at her shoes, so that her

thick brown lashes curled on to her cheeks. He was making her feel awkward again. She swallowed and tried once more.

'Should we go into the drawing-room, do you think?'

He stood aside without further preamble, and followed her into the room where she was instantly pounced upon by Sieske so that she could meet Wierd and see for herself that he was everything that her friend had said. He was indeed charming, and exactly right for Sieske. They made a handsome couple and a happy one too. Harriet suppressed a small pang of envy; it must be nice to be loved as Wierd so obviously loved Sieske. She drank the sherry Aede brought her and sat next to him during the meal which followed and joined in the laughter and talk, which was wholly concerned with the engagement party. It was discussed through the excellent soup, the *rolpens met rodekool*, the *poffertjes*—delicious morsels of dough fried in butter to an unbelievable lightness—and was only exhausted when an enormous bowl of fruit was put on the table. Harriet sat quietly while Aede peeled a peach for her, and listened to Dr Eijsinck's deep voice—he was discussing rose grafting with her hostess, who turned to her and said kindly, but in her own language,

'Harry, you must go and see Friso's garden, it is such a beautiful one.'

Aede repeated her words in English, and then went on in the same language.

'We went past your place this evening, Friso. I took Harriet for a run and we stopped while she admired your flowers.'

Harriet looked across the table at him then and smiled, and was puzzled to see his mobile mouth pulled down at the corners by a cynical smile, just as though he didn't in the least believe that she had a real fondness for flowers and gardens. When he said carelessly, 'By all means come and look round, Miss Slocombe,' he knew that he had given the invitation because there was nothing else he could do. She thanked him quietly, gave him a cool glance, and occupied herself with her peach. She took care to avoid him for the rest of the evening, an easy matter as it turned out, for Dr Van Minnen had discovered that she had only the sketchiest knowledge of Friesland's history, and set himself to rectify this gap in her education. It was only at the end of the evening that Dr Eijsinck spoke to her again and that was to wish her good night, and that a most casual one.

Later, in her pleasant little room, she sat brushing her hair and thinking about the evening. Something had gone wrong with her dream. It had seemed that kindly fate had intervened when she had met him again, but now she wasn't so sure, for that same fickle fate was showing her that dreams had no place in her workaday world. Harriet ground her even little teeth—even though he had a dozen beautiful girl-friends, he could at least pretend to like her. On reflection, though, she didn't think that he would bother to pretend about anything. She got into bed and turned out the light and lay in the comfortable darkness, wondering when she would see him again.

CHAPTER THREE

SHE awoke early to a sparkling April morning and the sound of church bells, and lay between sleeping and waking listening to them until Sieske came in, to sit on the end of the bed and talk happily about the previous evening.

'You enjoyed it too, Harry?' she asked anxiously.

Harriet sat up in bed—she was wearing a pink nightgown, a frivolous garment, all lace and ribbons. Her hair fell, straight and gold and shining, almost to her waist; she looked delightful.

'It was lovely,' she said warmly. 'I think your Wierd is a dear—you're going to be very happy.'

Sieske blushed. 'Yes, I know. You like Aede?'

Harriet nodded. 'Oh, yes. He's just like you, Sieske.'

'And Friso?'

Harriet said lightly, 'Well, we only said hullo and good-bye, you know. He's not quite what I expected.' She explained about the gravy stains and the permanent stoop, and Sieske giggled.

'Harry, how could you, and he is so hand-some, don't you think?'

Harriet said 'Very,' with a magnificent non-chalance.

'And so very rich,' Sieske went on.

'So I heard,' said Harriet, maintaining the nonchalance. 'How nice for him.'

Sieske curled her legs up under her and settled herself more comfortably. 'Also nice for his wife,' she remarked.

Harriet felt a sudden chill. 'Oh? Is he going to marry, then?' she asked, and wondered why the answer mattered so much.

Sieske laughed.

'Well, he will one day, I expect, but I think he enjoys being a...*vrijgezel*. I don't know the English—it is a man who is not yet married.'

'Bachelor,' said Harriet.

'Yes—well, he has many girl-friends, you see, but he does not love any of them.'

'How do you know that?' asked Harriet in a deceptively calm voice.

'I asked him,' said Sieske simply, 'and he told me. I should like him to be happy as Wierd is happy; and I would like you to be happy too, Harry,' she added disarmingly.

Harriet felt herself getting red in the face. 'But I am happy,' she cried. 'I've got what I wanted, haven't I? A sister's post, and—and—' The thought struck her that probably in twenty years' time she would still have that same sister's post. She shuddered. 'I'll get up,' she said, briskly cheerful to dispel the gloomy thought. But this she wasn't allowed to do; the family, it seemed, were going to church at nine o'clock, and had decided that the unfamiliar service and the long sermon wouldn't be of the least benefit to her. She was to stay in bed and go down to breakfast when she felt like it.

Sieske got up from the bed and stretched herself. 'We are back soon after ten, and Wierd comes to lunch. We will plan something nice to do.' She turned round as she reached the door. 'Go to sleep again, Harry.'

Harriet, however, had no desire for sleep. She lay staring at the roses on the wallpaper, contemplating her future with a complete lack of enthusiasm, and was suddenly struck by the fact that this was entirely due to the knowledge that Dr Eijsinck would have no part of it. The front door banged and she got out of bed to watch the Van Minnen family make their way down the street towards church, glad of the interruption of thoughts she didn't care to think. It wasn't quite nine o'clock; she slipped on the night-gown's matching peignoir and the rather ridiculous slippers which went with it, and made her way downstairs through the quiet old house to the dining-room.

Someone had thoughtfully drawn a small table

up to the soft warmth of the stove and laid it
with care, for cup, saucer and plate of a bright
brown earthenware, flanked by butter in a Delft
blue dish, stood invitingly ready. There was
coffee too, and a small basket full of an assort-
ment of bread, and grouped together, jam and
sausage and cheese. Harriet poured coffee,
buttered a crusty slice of bread with a lavish
hand and took a large satisfying bite. She had
lifted her coffee cup half-way to her lips when
the door opened.

'Where's everybody?' asked Dr Eijsinck,
without bothering to say good morning.
'Church?'

Harriet put down her cup. 'Yes,' she said,
with her mouth full. His glance flickered over
her and she went pink under it.

'Are you ill?' he asked politely, although his
look denied his words.

'Me? Ill? No.' If he chose to think of her as
a useless lazy creature, she thought furiously,
she for one would not enlighten him.

'Well, if you're not ill, you'd better come to
the surgery and hold down a brat with a bead
up his nose.'

'Certainly,' said Harriet, 'since you ask me
so nicely; but I must dress first.'

'Why? There's no one around who's interested in seeing you like that. The child's about
three; his mother's in the waiting room because

she's too frightened to hold him herself; and as for me, I assure you that I am quite unaffected.'

She didn't like the note of mockery—he was being deliberately tiresome! She put her cup back in its saucer, got up without a word and followed him down the passage to the surgery where she waited while he fetched the child from its mother. She took the little boy in capable arms and said, 'There, there,' in the soft, kind voice she used to anyone ill or afraid. He sniffed and gulped, and under her approving, 'There's a big man, then!' subsided into quietness punctuated by heaving breaths, so that she was able to lay him on the examination table without further ado, and steady his round head between her small firm hands. Dr Eijsinck, standing with speculum, probe and curved forceps ready to hand, grunted something she couldn't understand and switched on his head lamp.

'Will you be able to hold him with one arm?' she asked matter-of-factly.

He looked as though he was going to laugh, but his voice was mild enough as he replied. 'I believe I can manage, Miss Slocombe. He's quite small, and my arm is—er—large enough to suffice.'

He sprayed the tiny nostril carefully and got to work, his big hand manipulating the instruments with a surprising delicacy. While he worked he talked softly to his small patient; a meaningless jumble of words Harriet could make nothing of.

'Are you speaking Fries?' she wanted to know.

He didn't look up. 'Yes. . .I don't mean to be rude, but Atse here doesn't understand anything else at present.' He withdrew a bright blue bead from the small nose and Atse at once burst into tearful roars, the while his face was mopped up. Harriet scooped him up into her arms.

'Silly boy, it's all over.' She gave him a hug and he stopped his sobbing to look at her and say something. She returned his look in her turn. 'It's no good, Atse, I can't understand.'

Dr Eijsinck looked up from the sink where he was washing his hands.

'Allow me to translate. He is observing—as I daresay many other members of his sex have done before him—that you and your—er—dress are very beautiful.'

Harriet felt her cheeks grow hot, but she answered in a composed voice, 'What a lovely compliment—something to remember when I get home.'

The doctor had come to stand close to her and she handed him the little boy. 'Good-bye, Atse, I hope I see you again.' She shook the fat little hand, straightened the examination table, thumped up its pillow with a few brisk movements, and made for the door. She had opened it before Dr Eijsinck said quietly, 'Thank you for your help, Miss Slocombe.'

'Don't mention it,' she said airily, as she went through.

The breakfast table still looked very attractive; she plugged in the coffee pot and took another bite from her bread and butter. She was spreading a second slice with a generous wafer of cheese when the door opened again. Dr Eijsinck said from the doorway, 'I'm sorry I disturbed your breakfast.' And then, 'Is the coffee hot?'

She wiped a few crumbs away from her mouth, using a finger.

'Don't apologize, Doctor. . .and yes, thank you, the coffee is hot.'

There was a pause during which she remembered how unpleasant he had been. The look she cast him was undoubtedly a reflection of her thoughts, for he gave a sudden quizzical smile, said good-bye abruptly, and went.

They were having morning coffee when he arrived for the second time. He took the cup Mevrouw Van Minnen handed him and sat down unhurriedly; it seemed to Harriet, sitting by the window with Sieske, that he was very much one of the family. He was answering a great number of questions which Dr Van Minnen was putting to him, and Harriet thought what a pity it was she couldn't understand Dutch. Sieske must have read her thoughts, for she called across the room.

'Friso, were you called out?' and she spoke in English.

He replied in the same tongue. 'Yes, for my sins...an impacted fractured femur and premature twins.'

Sieske said quickly with a sideways look at Harriet, 'Don't forget Atse. Weren't you glad that Harry was here to help you?'

'Delighted,' he said in a dry voice, 'and so was Atse.'

Harriet, studying her coffee cup with a downbent head, was nonetheless aware that he was looking at her.

'So you didn't get to bed at all?' asked Aede.

'Er—no. I was on my way home when I encountered Atse and his mother; I was nearer here than my own place—it seemed logical to bring them with me. I'd forgotten that you would all be in church.'

Harriet abandoned the close scrutiny of her coffee cup. So he had been up all night; being a reasonable young woman she understood how he must have felt when he found her. And the coffee—he had asked if it was hot and she hadn't even asked him if he wanted a cup. How mean of her—she opened her mouth to say so, caught his eye and knew that he had guessed her intention. Before she could speak, he went on smoothly,

'I am indebted to—er—Harriet for her help; very competent help too.'

Mevrouw Van Minnen said something, Harriet had no idea what until she heard the word *koffie*. She opened her mouth once more, feeling guilty, but he was speaking before she could get a word out.

'What is Dr Eijsinck saying, Sieske?' she said softly.

Her friend gave a sympathetic giggle. 'Poor Harry, not understanding a word! He's explaining that he couldn't stay for the coffee you had ready for him because he had to go straight back to the twins.'

Harriet had only been in Holland a short time, but already she had realized that hospitality was a built-in feature of the Dutch character—to deny it to anyone was unthinkable. Mevrouw Van Minnen would have been upset. Friso was being magnanimous. The least she could do was to apologize and thank him for his thought-fulness.

He got up a few minutes later and strolled to the door with a casual parting word which embraced the whole company. She was too shy to get up too and follow him out—it might be days before she saw him again. He had banged the front door behind him when Sieske said urgently,

'There, I forgot to tell Friso about the flowers

for Wednesday! Harry, you're so much faster than I—run after him, will you? Tell him it's all right. He'll understand.'

Harriet reached the pavement just as he was getting into the car. He straightened when he saw her, and stood waiting, his hand still on the car door.

She said, short-breathed, 'Sieske asked me to give you a message. That it's all right about the flowers, and that you would understand.'

She stood looking at him and after a moment he gave a glimmer of a smile and said, 'Oh, yes. Of course. Thanks for reminding me.'

'I wanted to—It was lucky Sieske asked me. I'm so sorry about this morning—you know, the coffee. It was mean of me. I don't know why I did it.' She stopped and frowned, 'Yes, I do. You weren't very nice about me being in a dressing-gown, but of course I understand now, you must have been very tired if you were up all night—I daresay you wouldn't have minded so much if you had had a good night's sleep,' she finished ingenuously.

'No, I don't suppose I should,' he agreed gravely. He got into the car, said good-bye rather abruptly, and was gone, leaving her still uncertain as to whether he disliked her or not. It suddenly mattered very much that she should know, one way or the other.

They were immersed in plans when she got

back to the sitting-room. Wierd was coming to luncheon, reiterated Sieske; they would go for a drive, she and Wierd and Harriet and Aede. Dokkum, they decided, with an eye on Harriet's ignorance of the countryside, and then on to the coast to Oostmahorn, when the boat sailed for the small island of Schiermonnikoog.

They set out about two o'clock, Wierd and Sieske leading the way. It was glorious weather, although the blue sky was still pale and the wind keen. Harriet in a thick tweed suit and a head-scarf hoped she would be warm enough; the others seemed to take the wind for granted, but she hadn't got used to it. It was warm enough in the car, however, and Aede proved to be an excellent guide. By the time they had reached Dokkum, she had mastered a great deal of Friesian history and had even learnt—after a fashion—the Friesian National Anthem, although she thought the translation, 'Friesian blood, rise up and boil,' could be improved upon. The others were waiting for them in the little town, and she was taken at once to see the church of St Boniface and then the outside of the Town Hall, with a promise that she should be brought again so that she could see its beautiful, painted council room.

The coast, when they reached it, was a sur-prise and a contrast. Harriet found it difficult to reconcile the sleepy little town they had just left with the flat shores protected from the sea by the dykes built so patiently by the Friesians over the centuries. Land was still being reclaimed, too. She looked at the expanse of mud, and tried to imagine people living on it in a decade of time; she found it much more to her liking to think of the people who had lived in Dokkum hundreds of years ago, and had gone to the self-same church that she had just visited. She explained this to Aede, who listened carefully.

'Yes,' he said slowly, 'but if we had no dykes there would be no Dokkum.' Which was unanswerable. They turned for home soon after-wards and towards the end of the journey, Aede said, 'Here's Friso's village—his house is on the left.' They were approaching it from the other side at an angle which allowed her to catch a glimpse of the back of the house. It looked bigger somehow, perhaps because of the veranda stretching across its breadth. There were steps from it leading down to the garden, which she saw was a great deal larger than she had sup-posed. She peered through the high iron railing, but there was no one to see. He must be lonely, she thought, living there all by himself. The road curved, and they passed the entrance. At the moment, at any rate, he wasn't lonely—there were two cars parked by the door. Aede was going rather fast, so that she had only a glimpse; but with three car-crazy brothers, her knowledge

of cars was sound and up to date. One was a
Lotus Elan, the other a Marcos. It seemed that
Dr Eijsinck's friends like speed. Harriet thought
darkly of the beautiful brunette; she would look
just right behind the wheel of the Lotus. . . Her
thoughts were interrupted by Aede.

'Friso's got visitors. . . That man's cast iron;
he works for two most of the time, and when he's
not working he's off to Utrecht or Amsterdam or
Den Haag. Even if he stays home, there are
always people calling.'

Harriet watched the Friso of her dreams
fade—the Friso who would have loved her for
always; happy to be with her and no one else—
but this flesh and blood Friso didn't need her at
all. She went a little pink, remembering how she
had smiled at him when she had seen him for
the first time; he must have thought how silly
she was, or worse, how cheap. The pink turned
to red; she had been a fool. She resolved then
and there to stop dreaming and demonstrated
her resolution by turning to Aede and asking
intelligent questions about the reclamation of
land. Harriet listened with great attention to the
answers, not hearing them at all, but thinking
about Friso Eijsinck.

At breakfast the following morning, Harriet
learned that Sieske's two sisters would be
returning in time for tea. They had been visiting
their grandparents in Sneek, but now the Easter

holidays were over and they would be going back to high school Aede had gone back to hospital the previous evening; Dr Van Minnen had an unexpected appointment that afternoon; the question as it who should fetch them was debated over the rolls and coffee. Sieske supposed she could go, but there was the party to arrange.

Her father got to his feet. 'I'll telephone Friso,' he said, 'he's got no afternoon surgery, I'm certain. He'll go, and the girls simply love that car of his.'

He disappeared in the direction of his surgery, leaving his wife and Sieske, with Harriet as a willing listener, to plunge into the final details concerning the party. This fascinating discussion naturally led the three ladies upstairs to look at each other's dresses for the occasion; Sieske had brought a dress back from England—the blue of it matched her eyes; its straight classical lines made her look like a golden-haired goddess. They admired it at some length before repairing to Mevrouw Van Minnen's bedroom to watch approvingly while she held up the handsome black crepe gown she had bought in Leeuwarden. Evidently the party was to be an occasion for dressing up; Harriet was glad that she had packed the long white silk dress she had bought in a fit of extravagance a month or so previously. It had a lace bodice, square-necked

and short-sleeved, with a rich satin ribbon defin-
ing the high waistline. It would provide a good
foil for Sieske's dress without stealing any of
its limelight. She could see from Mevrouw Van
Minnen's satisfied nod that she thought so too.
They all went downstairs, satisfied that they had
already done a great deal towards making
Sieske's evening a success, and over cups of
coffee the menu for the buffet supper was finally
checked, for, said Mevrouw Van Minnen in
sudden, surprising English,

'We are beautiful ladies. . .but men eat too.'
She laughed at her efforts and looked as young
and pretty as her daughter.

'Will it be black ties?' Harriet wanted
to know.

Sieske nodded. 'Of course. We call it
Smoking—their clothes, I mean.'

Harriet giggled. 'How funny, though they
look nice whatever you call it.' Friso Eijsinck,
for instance, would look very nice indeed. . .

Harriet was sitting writing postcards at the
desk under the sitting-room window when she
heard a car draw up outside. It was the AC 428.
She watched the two girls and Dr Eijsinck get
out and cross the pavement to the front door;
the girls were obviously in high spirits, and so,
for that matter, was the doctor. Harriet, peeping
from her chair, thought that he looked at least
ten years younger and great fun. She returned

to her writing, and presently they all three
entered the room, bringing with them the unmistakable aura of longstanding friendship, which,
quite unintentionally, made her feel more of a
stranger than she had felt since she had arrived
in Holland, and because of this, her 'Good afternoon, Doctor', was rather stiff and she was all
the more annoyed when he said,

'Oh hullo—all alone again? I'd better intro-
duce you to these two.' He turned to the elder
of the girls.

'This is Maggina.' The girls shook hands and
Maggina said 'How do you do?'—she was like
her mother and Sieske, but without their vivid-
ness. Rather like a carbon copy, thought Harriet,
liking her.

'And Taeike,' said the doctor. She was fourteen or fifteen, and one saw she was going to
be quite lovely; now she was just a very pretty
girl, with a charming smile and nice manners.
She shook hands with Harriet, then went and
stood by Friso and slipped her hand under his
arm. He patted it absent-mindedly and asked
Harriet in a perfunctory manner if she had had
a busy day, but there was no need for her to
reply, for just then the rest of the family came
in and everybody talked at once and there was
nothing for her to do but to smile and withdraw
a little into the background. She looked up once
and found Dr Eijsinck watching her across the

room, with an expression on his face which she found hard to read, but he gave her no opportunity to do so, for the next moment he had taken his leave. She heard the front door bang and his car start up, but withstood the temptation to turn round and look out of the window.

Wednesday came, the day of the party, and with it a Land-Rover from Dr Eijsinck's house. It was driven by his gardener, and filled to overflowing with azaleas and polyanthus, and great bunches of irises and tulips and freesias. Harriet, helping to arrange them around the house, paused to study the complicated erection of flowers she had achieved in one corner of the drawing-room and to remark,

'I suppose Dr Eijsinck has a very large green house?'

It was Taeike who answered. 'He has three. I go many times—also to his house.'

Harriet twitched a branch of forsythia into its exact position before she answered, 'How nice.' It would be easy to find out a great deal about the doctor from Taeike, but she couldn't bring herself to do it. She asked instead,

'Tell me about your school, will you?' then listened to Taeike's polite, halting English, aware that the girl would have much rather talked about Friso Eijsinck.

Wierd came after tea, with more flowers, and sat talking to Dr Van Minnen until Sieske, who had gone upstairs to dress, came down again looking radiant. It was the signal for everyone else to go and dress too, leaving the pair of them to each other's company, to foregather presently in the drawing-room where they admired the plain gold rings the happy couple had exchanged. They would wear them until their marriage, when they would be transferred from their left hands to their right. It seemed to Harriet that this exchange of rings made everything rather solemn and binding. 'Plighting their troth,' she mused, and added her congratulations to everyone else's.

The guests arrived soon afterwards, and she circled the room with first one then the other of the Van Minnens, shaking hands and uttering her name with each handshake. A splendid idea—only some of the names were hard to remember. She was standing by the door, listening rather nervously to the *burgemeester*, a handsome man with an imposing presence who spoke the pedantic English she was beginning to associate with the educated Dutch, when Friso Eijsinck came in. She had been right. He looked—she sought for the right word and came up with eye-catching; but then so did the girl with him. A blonde this time, Harriet noted, watching her while she smiled attentively at her companion, and wearing a dress straight out of *Harpers & Queen*. In her efforts to prevent a

scowl of envy, Harriet smiled even more brilli-
antly and gazed at the *burgemeester* with such
a look of absorbed attention that he embarked
upon a monologue, and a very knowledgeable
one, about the various theatres he had visited
when he was last in London. It was fortunate
that he didn't expect an answer, for Harriet was
abysmally ignorant about social life in the great
metropolis, and was about to say so, when he
paused for breath and Friso said from behind her,

   'Good evening, Miss Slocombe. . .*burgemeester.*'

He shook hands with them both, and the *burgemeester* said,

   'I was just telling this charming young lady
how much I enjoyed "The Mousetrap"!' He
turned to Harriet. 'I also went to see "Cats".'
He coughed. 'You've seen it, of course, Miss
Slocombe?'

Both men were looking down at her, the
speaker with a look of polite inquiry, Dr Eijsinck
with a decided twinkle in his grey eyes. Her
colour deepened. 'Well, no. You see I live in a
very small village on the edge of Dartmoor. I. . .I
don't go to London often.' She forbore to mention that she hadn't been there for at least five
years. She withdrew her gaze from the older
man and looked quickly at the doctor, whose
face was a mask of polite interest; all the same,
she was very well aware that he was laughing

at her. She opened her eyes very wide and said with hauteur, 'Even if I lived in London I think it would be unlikely that I should go to see "Cats". I'm not very with-it, I'm afraid.'

She allowed her long curling lashes to sweep down on to her cheeks for just a sufficient length of time for her two companions to note that they were real. The *burgemeester*, who was really rather a dear, allowed a discreet eye to rove over her person. He said with elderly gallantry,

'I think that you are most delightfully with-it, Miss Slocombe. I hope that I shall see more of you before you return to that village of yours. And now take her away, Friso, for I am sure that was your reason for joining us.'

There was nothing to do but smile, and, very conscious of Friso's hand on her arm, allow herself to be guided across the room. Once out of earshot, however, she stood still and said,

'I'll be quite all right here, Doctor. I'm sure there are a great many people to whom you wish to talk.' She looked pointedly through the open double doors into the dining-room, where the beautiful blonde, glass in hand, was holding court. Somebody had started the record-player; Sieske started to dance and half a dozen couples joined them. Her companion, without bothering to answer her, swung Harriet on to the impromptu dance floor. He danced well, with a complete lack of tiresome mannerisms. Harriet,

who was a good dancer herself, would have been
happy to have remained as his partner for the
rest of the evening, but in fact it was long after
midnight before he came near her again. She
was perched on the bottom stair, between two
of Aede's friends, listening to their account of
life on the wards in a Rotterdam hospital where
they were housemen. She saw him standing in
the open doorway of the drawing-room across
the hall, watching them. After a minute he
started to cross the hall, taking care that both
young men saw his approach. When he was near
enough, he said smoothly,

'Harriet, I have looked for you everywhere.'
He glanced at the two young men with a smile
of charm and authority which brought them to
their feet with a cheerful 'Very well, sir,' and
an equally cheerful 'See you later' for Harriet
who found herself alone on the staircase; but not
for long, for Dr Eijsinck folded himself into the
space beside her, taking up the lion's share of
it with his bulk. Harriet was annoyed to feel a
thrill of pleasure at his closeness and in an effort
to ignore it, said crossly,

'You haven't been looking for me everywhere—you must have seen me dozens of times
in the last hour or so. And why did you send
those two boys away? I wanted them to stay.'

He stretched out his long legs. 'Yes, I thought
you would,' he said complacently. 'That's why.'

Harriet's bosom heaved with an emotion she didn't bother to define; she turned furious blue eyes to meet his lazily smiling ones. 'Well,' she uttered at length, and then again, 'Well!'

'At a loss for words?' he asked kindly, to madden her. She turned her head away, and smiled at Taeike who was wandering across the hall, and was on the point of calling her when he said softly, 'No, Harry, I want to talk to you.' His voice sounded different—firm and gentle. She looked at him and went slowly pink under the look on his face; he was smiling too—the smile was different too. He studied her for a minute and then said mildly, 'That's better; you usually look at me as though I were a rather unspeakable drain.'

She gave a little splutter of laughter at that and then frowned fiercely to show him that she hadn't meant it. 'Excepting the first time we met,' he continued, ignoring the frown. 'You looked at me then as though you were—er—glad to see me.'

She managed to look away at last, and despite the sudden thudding of her heart said steadily, 'I thought you were someone I. . .knew.'

'That's not quite true, is it?'

Not looking at him made it easier to regain a level head. He hadn't said that he had been glad to see her; and what about the brunette and the exotic blonde who had accompanied him that evening? And what had Aede said? That Friso had a great many girlfriends—Sieske had said it too. Harriet had no intention of being one of the many. She said in the same steady voice,

'Not quite true, no. But it answers your question well enough.'

She looked at him then, to find only amusement on his face, perhaps she had been mistaken after all. He held out a hand. 'Let's dance,' he said.

They circled the room once before he drew her out on to the verandah. The night was surprisingly mild, wind still and very dark. They stood looking out over the unseen garden; the faint clean smell of grass, mingled with the tang of tulips and the heavier scent of the hyacinths, made the air a delight. The music had stopped, to be replaced by a babble of voices until presently a new record was put on—it was 'If you go away' and a man was singing. Harriet listened to the words—they made her feel sad, even though they were only part of a song. Friso Eijsinck, very close beside her, said softly,

'You like this song.' It was a statement, not a question.

'Yes.'

'You think it is possible for a man to feel like that about a woman?'

'Yes,' said Harriet. Regrettably, her conversational powers had deserted her; perhaps a good thing, for she was having difficulty with her breathing.

'It expresses sentiments which I do not think I can improve upon,' said Dr Eijsinck thoughtfully, 'unless it is by doing this. . .'

She was caught, turned and held close—and then kissed. She had been kissed before, but never in this fashion. Against all common sense, she kissed him back. When she drew away he loosened his hold at once, but without releasing her, and said over her shoulder,

'Hullo, Taeike.'

Harriet, still within the circle of his arm, glimpsed her standing in the doorway for a brief moment before she turned on her heel and went inside. She had said nothing at all, but she had broken the spell; she told herself that she was glad, for she had so nearly allowed herself to be carried away. She said lightly,

'It's getting chilly—shall we go inside?' and led the way back to the drawing-room without looking at him. She was at once whisked off to dance, and Friso didn't seek her out again, only towards the end of the evening she saw his broad back disappearing through the door, and when she searched the room, the beautiful blonde had gone too.

It was while she was helping to restore some sort of order to the rooms after the last guest had gone that Harriet finally admitted to herself that she had fallen in love with Friso Eijsinck; not the perfect Friso of her dream, but this man of whom she knew nothing; who barely spoke to her, and when he did, left her uncertain as to whether he even liked her. She stacked some plates carefully—probably he didn't—his kiss on the verandah had been almost certainly prompted by the sweet-smelling garden and the song. . .and almost as certainly he would have forgotten it by now. She wished with all her heart that she could do the same.

CHAPTER FOUR

IT seemed very quiet on Thursday; Wierd, who was a pathologist and worked for a big drug firm outside Delft, had left early; so had Aede; neither of them would be back again for at least a week, but Sieske, sitting on the end of Harriet's bed for a rather sleepy morning gossip, told her that Wierd had suggested that the two girls should go down to Delft on Monday; he would be free in the afternoon, and it was a chance for Harriet to see something of Holland.

'Very nice,' said Harriet, 'but I'd love to poke around on my own. Would you mind? You could both meet me somewhere.'

Sieske protested at this until Harriet said, 'Then I shan't come.' She liked Sieske very much, and Wierd was great fun, but she remembered the old adage 'Two's company, three's none'. Besides, it would be good for her to go on her own. She smiled persuasively at her friend, and got her own way.

They went to Sneek in the afternoon, to visit Sieske's grandparents. Sieske drove the Mini she and her mother shared between them, with Harriet beside her, and Mevrouw Van Minnen

dozing comfortable in the back. They took the
narrow country roads, through small villages,
each with its own church and café, and less fre-
quently, a solitary shop, with rows of *klompen*
on either side of the door and a great many
advertisements in the windows for Van Nelle's
tea and Niemeijer's coffee and the more familiar
washing powders and Blue Band. Sneek, when
they reached it, was smaller than she had
expected, and very quiet. Sieske explained that
the best time to visit it was during the sailing
week in August, when it was packed with visitors, but it was too early in the year for the boats
to be out on Sneekermeer, although the more
hardy were to be found at week-ends, wrapped
warmly against the wind, enjoying the luxury of
an almost empty lake.

Sieske's grandparents lived close by the
Water Gate, in a house as old and charming as
their son's; they had, of course, been at the party
the previous evening, but had gone home early.
Now they settled down comfortably to mull over
every aspect of the guests' clothes, views and
appearance, and this naturally led to a not
unkindly gossip about their various friends, and
finally, over cups of tea, praise of Mevrouw Van
Minnen for having arranged such a memorable
evening. Harriet didn't understand the half of it,
but there was a great deal to look at in the room,
and Sieske translated as much as possible of the

conversation, and presently old Mijnheer Van Minnen came and sat beside her, and talked, rather hesitantly, in English. He asked a great many questions and expressed surprise that she was not married, or at least engaged.

'Perhaps you will find a husband here, Harriet,' he said. She felt herself go pink under his sharp old eyes and was glad that they got up to go before she needed to answer.

Maggina and Taeike were home when they got back; they were tired and rather cross and didn't talk much, and after the evening meal they went to the small room at the back of the house where they studied their school books without the temptations of the radio or television, leaving their elders to sit and talk in desultory fashion until they dispersed, by common consent to an early bed.

The next morning at breakfast, Harriet asked, rather diffidently, if she might help in the morning surgery. 'I could look out the cards for you, Doctor, and clear up things—that's if no one minds.'

She looked round the table. Sieske, she knew, was going to the dressmakers, the girls had already left for school. . .she turned back to the doctor, who smiled and said, 'Yes, Harriet, you would be a real help, but you must not feel that because you do it today, that you have to do it every day.'

The waiting room was full; it was, Harriet thought, very like Out-Patients in hospital. The fact that she was unable to understand a word of what was being said made very little difference. Cut fingers and earache and varicose ulcers were the same in any language. The plump rosy-cheeked babies cried in exactly the same way as did the babies at home, and the small boys were just as bent on having their own way. The last patient came and went, and she cleared up, closed the filing cabinets and went back through the door into the house, and if she felt disappointment at not seeing Dr Eijsinck, she didn't admit it to herself.

They went to the Planetarium in the afternoon; there was no one there but herself and Sieske and the curator, who explained the complexity of nails in the little attic, and answered her questions in schoolmaster's English. She had no doubt at all that he would have answered her just as easily and fluently in French or German. They went back downstairs into the small back room where the solar system revolved, year after year, around the blue wooden ceiling. It was a small house; she imagined it centuries earlier, not very well furnished, but cosy. Like so many other houses in Holland, it became home the moment you entered the front door. But perhaps, she reflected, that only applied to the old houses she had been in; she had had no opportunity to visit anything modern and didn't particularly want to. She wondered, fleetingly, if she would be given the opportunity to see inside Dr Eijsinck's house. The possibility seemed remote.

It was the next morning, during their early morning gossip, that Sieske said, 'Let's go over to Friso's house this afternoon; Father is on call this week-end, and Mother will stay with him, and Maggina and Taeike are going to some friends. There's an old bike you can have.' She looked inquiringly at Harriet, who said, in a neutral voice,

'That sounds fun, but won't he mind?'

'He won't be there; it's his week-end off, and he said something about going to The Hague.'

Harriet said slowly, through an aching disappointment, 'I'd love to go.' It would, after all, be something, just to see his garden.

They set off after lunch, laughing a good deal, for the bicycle which had been found for Harriet was an old-fashioned model, with high handlebars and a saddle to match. She felt like Queen Victoria at her most dignified until she nearly fell off when she idly back-pedalled. She had quite forgotten that was how the brakes worked.

There was a narrow paved path running beside the road to the village; for the exclusive use of cyclists, it made the journey much less hazardous for Harriet, who felt a keen urge to veer to the left. The path was uneven, and dropped a couple of feet into a ditch on its other side, so it was just as well that she had no traffic problems; besides, there was a great deal to look at and exclaim over. The April sun was warm and in its light the countryside looked as though it had been newly painted; only the sky was still a remote, pale blue, and the wind, the ever-present wind, chilled everything it touched. Harriet, despite her thick polo-necked sweater and slacks, shivered, to be warmed by the sight of the iron gates of Friso's house, their gilded spear-headed tops shining in the sun, and standing invitingly open. The drive was short and straight, to end in a generous sweep of smooth gravel before the front of the house before it divided, to disappear round either corner. Sieske led the way to the left-hand fork. Harriet, following more slowly, surveyed the solid front door, with its imposing knocker and beautiful fanlight, and longed to get off her bike and go inside. There were three long windows before she reached the corner; she could just glimpse their draped pelmets and rich, heavy curtains; the windows continued along the side of the house too, and there was a small stone balustraded stair disappearing to a basement she could not see.

Sieske had disappeared and Harriet found her standing on the vast gravelled space behind the house. She had propped her machine against the stone balustrade which separated it from the garden below, and Harriet put hers carefully beside it and turned to look her fill. The veranda she had seen from Aede's car ran the full width of the house behind them, a fine tracery of wrought iron, with wide floor-length windows opening on to it from the house, and a delicate stair leading to the gravel, from whose centre another stone stair led to the garden. It was a perfect example of Dutch formality; an exact rectangle enclosed by a yew hedge clipped to perfection, filled with a geometrical design of flowers in carefully matched or contrasting colours bordered by green velvet turf. There was a rectangular pool in its centre, with a flagstone path running around it, and a group of small stone children ringing a small fountain as its focal point. Harriet leaned comfortably over the stonework, looking at it all, and said at length,

'If I lived here, with this garden, I should never want to go anywhere else so long as I lived,' and then flushed pinkly in case Sieske misunderstood. Apparently she hadn't, for she said merely,

'Yes, it is beautiful, and old too. Friso's ancestor, the one who built the house, made the garden—it's not been changed since.' She turned away and said, 'Let's go and find Jan—he's the gardener—and tell him we're here.' She led the way along a narrow path at right angles to the house; it had turf borders and dense shrubbery on either side.

'This leads to the greenhouses,' explained Sieske. 'I'll go on ahead, shall I, and then come back for you.'

Left alone, Harriet slowed her steps. It was warm and sheltered and very quiet. The path curled and curled again and then divided. She took the left-hand fork and came almost immediately into a small open space, with a potting shed in one corner with a wheel-barrow outside it. Friso Eijsinck was sitting on its handle, filling a pipe. He got to his feet and said 'Hullo,' in a quite unsurprised way, and smiled at her so that her heart thumped against her ribs and she could barely muster breath to say 'Hullo' too, and then stupidly, 'You're in The Hague.'

'I changed my mind,' he said easily. 'Come and sit down.'

'Sieske's gone to speak to your gardener.' She had retrieved her breath; all the same, she thought she would stay where she was. 'I hope it's convenient. . .we didn't think you would be home, Doctor Eijsinck.'

Her voice sounded stiff even to her own ears, as it apparently did to her listener's, for he said invitingly, 'Try calling me Friso, and stop playing at Haughty Harry with me. I'm not a carefree young houseman, you know—you're quite safe.'

She stared at him, beautiful eyes blazing beneath knitted brows, her mouth slightly open while she sought for words. 'Well,' she managed, 'of all the...you...you...' A thought struck her. 'How did you know about Haughty Harry?' she demanded.

He said smoothly, 'Your fame went before you. Sieske painted a very true picture of you— I should have recognized you anywhere.' He patted the other handle of the wheelbarrow. 'Come and sit down.' She did as she was bid this time, and he said, 'That's better; I do dislike saying everything twice.'

She asked at once, for she had to know, 'Did you know who I was—I mean that day I was waiting on the pavement...'

'Yes, of course. And you recognized me, didn't you, although you didn't know me.'

She scuffled her feet in the soft earthy ground and wondered exactly what he meant. She would like to know. She had opened her mouth to ask when Sieske's voice, quite close, called, 'Harry, where are you?' She appeared beside them before they could reply and said comfortably,

'There you are—how nice that you found Friso; I stopped to look at these orchids of yours, Friso. They're gorgeous.'

She sat down on the wheelbarrow handle which he had vacated, and he went to sit on a chopping block. It was typical of the man, thought Harriet, that he contrived to look well-dressed in an open-necked shirt and corduroys and Wellingtons. He looked up and caught her eye, and she said in a hurry, 'Oh, do you grow orchids? How interesting,' and was sorry she had spoken, for he immediately began to talk about paphiopedilums and odontoglossums, only pausing to say, 'But of course you would know all about them, Harriet.'

She gave him a level look and said flatly, 'No. I just like gardens.'

'Ah, yes, of course,' he remarked blandly, and got to his feet. 'And I shall be delighted to show you this one.'

They set off, the three of them, shortly to be joined by two dogs, who appeared silently from the shrubbery and padded along, one each side of the doctor who was leading the way. 'J. B.,' he introduced the bulldog with a casual wave of his hand, and when Harriet said 'Hullo, J. B.', the noble animal gave her a considered glance and plodded on. His canine companion was, however, of a quite different character; due perhaps to his peculiar appearance. He seemed to be all tail, with a long thin body and a small pointed foxy face with eyes of melting softness. He watched his master eagerly and when the doctor said 'This is Flotsam' danced around Harriet with a great show of good fellowship.

'Nice dog,' said Harriet, 'but what a funny name.'

'Yes, isn't it?' remarked Sieske, 'but it's just right, you see, because Friso found. . .' she was quietly interrupted.

'Shall we go round the Dutch garden first? It's by far the best thing to see.'

They wandered around, taking their time, especially Harriet, who was inclined to go off on little trips of her own to get a closer view of anything which might have caught her eye. Her enthusiasm was shared by Flotsam who behaved as though he was seeing everything for the first time and was enraptured by it; Harriet bent down and pulled gently at a long feathery ear—he really was an unusual-looking dog, not at all the sort of animal she would expect to find. Her thoughts were interrupted by Friso saying,

'Sieske, would you go into the house and tell Anna to have tea for the three of us—I'll take Harriet to see the garden room and we'll join you in a few minutes.' He had been strolling along with an arm flung around Sieske's shoulders, but withdrew it now, and gave her a gentle push. 'If your mother is expecting you home you can telephone her at the same time.'

Harriet watched her friend disappear in the direction of the house, and then, because Friso was staring at her, burst into speech.

'A garden room? It sounds delightful. Where

is it? Do we go the same way as Sieske?'

She should have held her tongue, for he came very close and took hold of her hand and kissed her, very lightly, on her cheek, then said, laughing a little, 'No, we go down here,' and drew her along a very narrow path burrowing itself through the shrubbery. It was surprisingly short and ended opposite the small stone stairs she had passed earlier in the afternoon. They went down it, still hand in hand, with the dogs close at their heels, and Friso opened the thick wooden door on to a room lighted by a row of little windows under the verandah. It was dim and cool inside, with rows of shelves along its white-washed walls, piled with a comfortable clutter of flower pots, seed trays, balls of string and watering cans. There was a heavy wooden table against one wall and a variety of shabby basket chairs, plumply upholstered and well cushioned. Along the other wall there was a stone trough full with a great variety of ferns, their scent delicious and faintly damp.

Harriet looked around her. 'It's nice,' she said slowly, 'to be here, on a warm summer day, arranging the flowers for the house. . .' She stopped and blushed, for she hadn't meant to say that at all, but Friso said smoothly, as though he hadn't heard, 'My mother used to bring me here when I was a very small boy. I sat and watched her while she filled the vases; she did it very well.'

Harriet looked up and met his calm grey eyes, her own holding the question she didn't like to voice; he answered it as though she had spoken. 'She's in Curaçao, with my young brother; he's Medical Superintendent at the hospital there. He's been married for a couple of years and they had a little girl a few months ago; my mother went to the christening.' He went on deliberately, 'I also have a sister. She's married too, and lives in Geneva.'

Harriet bent down and tickled Flotsam's chin, then said uncertainly, 'I'm glad you have a family.'

'Now why should you say that?' he wanted to know. She found herself telling him about the stained waistcoat and the stoop and the harassed expression, then peeped at him to see if he was laughing, and was surprised to find that he wasn't. 'And were you sorry for me?' he asked gravely.

'Well, yes,' said Harriet, and he went on, 'But not any more.'

'No.' She felt foolish and a bit cross, mostly with herself. 'How can I be sorry for you when you have a lovely home and a family and a gorgeous car,' she paused, 'and—and beautiful girl-friends.'

He gave a great shout of laughter, and she

said with a certain peevishness, 'I'm glad you find it amusing,' and started to walk towards the door, but he got there first and stood in front of it, blocking it entirely, looking down at her, smiling.

'You're beautiful too, Harriet. Shall I add you to my collection of girl-friends?'

She stood very still, waiting for the feeling of anger which didn't come; only a sudden wish to burst into tears followed by the urgent desire to toss off some lighthearted reply. For the life of her, she couldn't think of one, and was still desperately searching when he said gently, 'I'm sorry, Harriet—I had forgotten that you aren't like anyone else.' He opened the door and whistled to the dogs, 'Let's have tea,' he said in a perfectly ordinary voice.

They entered the house from the veranda. The room, she supposed, was the drawing-room; it was very large and high-ceilinged, the walls were painted white and intricately gilded, there was a great crystal chandelier hanging from the centre of the ceiling, and miniature ones spaced along the walls. The floor-length curtains were of deep rose velvet, fringed and braided and elaborately swathed; they matched the carpet and the cut velvet of some of the chairs and the enormous couches on either side of the hooded fireplace, but the remainder of the easy chairs and the window cushions were covered in a pale chintz, which somehow turned the rather formal room into a very habitable one. Harriet had stopped just inside the french window; it wasn't the sort of room to be walked through unheeding, but Friso said briskly,

'This is the salon—drawing-room you would say, I think. We always have tea in the small parlour—it's cosier.'

He led the way to a door set in the wall and opened it for her to go in. The room was indeed small and cosy compared with the rather grand room they had just left; it was panelled in some wood Harriet didn't recognize and was carpeted in a rich claret colour which was echoed in the brocade curtains at the windows. There were several high-backed, winged chairs, and a couple of William and Mary tallbacks flanking a sofa table. Harriet saw that they were all old, beautifully cared for, and used constantly. Sieske, who was curled up in a chair by the small fireplace, put down the magazine she was reading.

'I told Anna that we would ring for tea'— she waved a hand at the small table beside her, already burdened with plates of biscuits and tiny iced cakes and paperthin sandwiches; apparently Friso liked more than a cup of tea in the afternoon. He walked across the room now, and pulled the old-fashioned bell rope, at the same time saying,

'Sit down, Harriet,' and took a seat himself

near Sieske and asked her, 'Are you going to Delft in the Mini?'

Sieske put down her magazine.

'Yes. Oh, Friso, will you come too—I mean, we could all go in your car.'

He hesitated before he replied, so that Harriet was filled with a sudden excitement that he would, then he said coolly, 'Sorry. I'm pretty sure to be busy, and there's the baby clinic in the afternoon.' He stretched out his vast person, so that he filled the not inconsiderable chair he sat in, and started to talk about nothing at all, and continued to do so, most entertainingly, all through tea. They got up to go presently, and Harriet reflected that he hadn't suggested that she might like to see at least some of his house. But he made no such suggestion, nor did he mention another visit, but walked to the gates with them and said '*Tot ziens*' in a casual way, which was, she had already gathered, the Dutch way of saying See you soon. They were some yards from the gate when he bellowed something at Sieske, who looked over her shoulder and shouted back. Harriet would have liked to look back at him too, but she recognized her limitations as a cyclist; to risk falling flat on her face would have ruined a not altogether successful afternoon. She said to Sieske, who was beside her again, 'He sounded as though he was swearing great oaths!'

Sieske laughed. 'Dutch is perhaps a little difficult. Friso merely said that he would call for us
tomorrow morning and take us to church.'

Harriet rang her bell for no reason at all. 'Not
me?' she asked.

'Yes, of course, you. You and me. Mother
will stay in case there are calls for Father. I do
not know about Maggina and Taeike; I suppose
if they want to come, they can.' She fell to talking about the garden, and Friso's name wasn't
mentioned again.

Harriet dressed with care the next morning.
Her thin wool dress and coat were almost new
and a delicious shade of almond green. They
became her mightily; so did the silk turban with
its ends tied in a jaunty knot in the nape of her
neck; her shoes were good ones and matched
her gloves and handbag. She applied Miss Dior
with thoughtful care and surveyed herself in the
long mirror between the windows; even her critical eye approved of what it saw. She nodded at
her reflection and went downstairs; the desire to
impress Dr Eijsinck with the knowledge that she
was no penniless dowd working powerfully
within her. Sieske was in the sitting-room, tele-
phoning Wierd; she looked up as Harriet went
in, raised her eyebrows and made a feminine
sound of appreciation, echoed by Maggina and
Taeike, who appeared, hatted and gloved, in the
doorway.

Sieske had rung off and was about to speak when the front door was opened by a powerful arm and Friso joined them. He gave them a collective good morning, bestowed a brief disinterested glance on Harriet, much as a man would look at yesterday's newspaper, and disappeared in the direction of the surgery. He reappeared a moment later, agreed casually to Taeike's urgent request to sit by him in front, and opened the door; as they filed through, he said, feelingly, 'Great heavens, four of you!' There was laughter from the Van Minnens and a polite smile from Harriet; after all, he had suggested it, hadn't he? The ill-conceived idea that she should cry off with a splitting headache was wrecked at birth by his compelling hand helping her far more carefully than was necessary, into the car.

The church was large, too large for the size of the village, but nonetheless surprisingly full. Dr Eijsinck's pew was in the very front; it had elaborately carved ends which bore his name written in copper plate on a little white card fixed into a brass holder. He stood, completely at ease, while they all filed past him. Taeike had hung back, but had had to go in first, looking sulky; Maggina went next, then Sieske, who took Harriet's hand and tugged it gently. The doctor settled himself in the remaining space; there seemed to be a great deal of him at such close quarters. He found the hymn for her in a beauti-

ful leather-bound book he produced from a
pocket, while Sieske explained about not kneel-
ing and sitting down to sing and to pray. Harriet
felt faintly confused, especially as she wasn't
attending very much to Sieske. How could she,
with Friso sitting beside her?

Even though she didn't understand a word of
the service, she enjoyed it. The doctor and Sieske
took care to point out how far they had got in
the incomprehensible book she held as she sat
between them, listening to Sieske's pretty voice
singing, and to the doctor's deep one, booming
its way unselfconsciously through the hymns.
The sermon was long, but the *dominee*, an enormous white-haired man with a compelling voice,
fascinated her. She had the impression that he
was haranguing the congregation about their
misdeeds, but a cautious glance around showed
nothing but rows of guiltless faces—either they
hid their feelings well, or he was unnecessarily
stern. But whatever he was his voice was beautiful; it rolled around the church, helped by the
magnificent sounding board above his head, and
she wished she understood him.

She had been warned beforehand about the
two collections; she had her two *guldens* ready
as the elders advanced down the aisle, but then
her eye caught the notes in the doctor's hands—
they were almost hidden, but she thought that
they were for ten *gulden*. She looked at Sieske,

but she was bending over to pick up a glove. The doctor's enormous hand took her bag from her, extracted the two *gulden* pieces, and put one in each of her hands. He said nothing, but he smiled, his grey eyes twinkling, so that she found herself smiling back at him. Just for that moment they seemed to have known each other for ever.

It seemed that they were to go back to Friso's house after church; a few people were coming in for drinks; it was all very like life in the village at home. Harriet followed the others through the main door into the tiled hall, and allowed a small neat man with a wrinkled face to remove her coat and take her gloves, and then shook hands with him when Maggina introduced him as Wim without explaining who he was. He didn't follow them into the drawing-room, so presumably he was the manservant Aede had mentioned. She lingered for a moment at the door; she would have dearly liked to have explored the hall and the doors on either side of it, and still more, the carved staircase curving up to the floor above. There were a number of portraits on the walls too. She turned reluctantly to encounter the vast expanse of the doctor's waistcoat, and spoke to it with a hint of apology. 'I was just looking at the hall. It's rather—rather beautiful.' She blushed fiercely; even to her own ears the remark had sounded pretentious. 'Not that I know anything about it,' she added, inadequately, making it worse.

He stood aside for her to enter the room and said politely, 'I'm glad you like it. Come and have a glass of sherry,' and ushered her across the expanse of carpet to where the others were sitting. She had barely taken two sips when the door opened again, and the *dominee* came in, followed by several other people who apparently were on terms of good friendship with Friso. Harriet shook hands with them rather shyly, and was relieved when they immediately spoke in English, showing a kindly interest in her which she found very pleasant, if surprising. She was passed from one to other little group until she fetched up by the *dominee*, who asked a great many questions in quite perfect and beautifully spoken English, and only interrupted himself when the lantern clock on the wall beside him struck the hour in a delicate faraway fashion. 'So late!' he exclaimed, 'I must go, but with regret. We must meet again before you return, Miss Slocombe.' He engulfed her hand and shook it so that the bones protested and went away, to be replaced at once by an elegantly dressed little woman, who wanted to know, surprisingly, if Marks and Spencer were still selling those rather nice quilted dressing-gowns. . .she had bought one on her last visit to London; she would certainly get another if they were still available. Harriet, who did a good deal of her own shopping there, was able to give her the news that they were, and the absorbing topic of clothes kept them happily occupied until there was a general movement of departure.

Harriet found herself going through the door with the doctor, hazily uncertain as to how this had happened; she had thought that she was surrounded by other people; they appeared to have melted away. They paused on the step outside, watching everyone sort themselves into their cars. There was another car there now, a dark blue Bentley, with Wim sitting in the driving seat. She said without much thought, 'Is that your car, too, the Bentley?' She glanced up at him, to encounter a cool glance from the grey eyes.

'Yes. Wim will take you back. I'm sorry that I cannot, but I have guests for luncheon.' He put his hands in his pockets, lounging against the side of the door. 'By the way,' he said, 'you look very smart—I'm much impressed. But then I was meant to be, was I not, Harriet?'

She took her glove off, and then put it on again with care; her voice shook only a little when she replied, 'How detestable you are! I hope I shan't see you again, Dr Eijsinck.' She started to walk towards the car, and he walked with her.

'You're a shocking liar,' he remarked cheerfully. He saw them all into the car, ignoring Taeike's still sulky face, then put his head through the open window next to Harriet.

'I should have asked you to lunch, Harriet, then you could have met the brunette.' He grinned at her. Before she could think of an answer the car had started.

'What did he mean?' asked Taeike sharply. Harriet was far too busy with her own thoughts to notice the edge of the girl's voice. 'Oh, it was just a joke,' she said carefully, and fell to talking about the various people she had met.

CHAPTER FIVE

THEY set off for Delft the following morning, shortly after breakfast; a meal during which each member of the family had added his or her quota to the list of sights that Harriet simply had to see. She wrote them down in her neat handwriting with a pen borrowed from Dr Van Minnen, on a leaf torn from his pocket-book. It was a lengthy list by the time she had finished it; she looked up to make some laughing remark and encountered Taeike's stare from the other side of the table. For a brief, unbelieving second Harriet thought she saw hate in the pretty little face, and then told herself she was mistaken as Taeike's face broke into a sweet smile as she said in her deliberate English, 'I hope you have a lovely day, Harriet.'

They went over the Afsluitdijk, Sieske sending the Mini racing along its length while she pointed out the opposite coast and explained about the *dijk*. Harriet listened and looked at the quiet water lapping at the *dijk*'s edge, and watched the birds pottering along between the stones of the *dijk* itself. It was all very quiet and peaceful. There were very few cars, and those tore past them, their only aim to get to the other side as quickly as possible. They went through the giant sluices and were on dry land again; pretty enough, but not to be compared with Friesland. She told Sieske so, to have her remark greeted with delight.

'You speak like a true Friesian,' she glanced sideways at Harriet. 'I believe you like my country, do you not?'

'Very much,' said Harriet. She was thinking of Friso Eijsinck.

'And the people?' went on Sieske.

'I like them too,' said Harriet. She went pink and turned a flurried attention to the landscape, which unfortunately hardly merited any comment, so she fell back on the safe and ever-engrossing topic of her friend's wedding, and if Sieske thought that the subject had been changed rather suddenly, she gave no sign.

They had plenty of time. Wierd was to meet them after lunch, and it was barely half past nine when they reached the further shore. Sieske decided to take the by-roads across the *polders*; it would give Harriet a chance to see the new farms the Government had built on the reclaimed land. The country was neat and orderly and new to the point of bareness, but the farms looked prosperous and well cared for, but presently they left the *polders* behind and in due time reached Broekop-Langendijk, much more to Harriet's liking, for it was nothing but a complex of canals criss-crossing in all directions, held together by a great many bridges. The canals were alive with a number of small boats and an occasional large one—to her enchanted eye it looked like the backdrop to some gigantic musical show. Sieske, who knew the way very well, crossed the main road just above Alkmaar and took the road to the dunes until it emerged on the other side of the Velsen tunnel and they were back on the main road again. But now there was a great deal to see; the bulb-fields were showing their colours, not perhaps at their perfection, but none-theless a delight to the eye. Harriet gazed at everything in sight and never stopped asking questions, which Sieske, her eyes on the road, answered with great good nature and in some detail.

They parked the car in a narrow cobbled street in Delft; its bonnet hanging precariously over the canal beside it. Harriet eyed the quiet water below; the car wheels were only a few inches from the edge—but apparently everyone parked in the same manner; it made more room, Sieske explained. They strolled to the market place, and found a tiny coffee shop behind a pastrycook's, and drank their coffee and made their plans.

'I wish you'd come with us this afternoon,' said Sieske for the hundredth time.

Harriet shook her head. 'I'd love to potter off

by myself if you don't mind, Sieske. I'll meet you for tea—only write down the name of the café.'

Presently they wandered off, standing to gaze at canals and bridges and old houses, of which there were a great many; until they stopped for lunch in the courtyard of a small restaurant next to the Prinsenhof Museum. Here they parted, Sieske to meet Wierd, Harriet to explore the museum so conveniently close by. Her afternoon went too quickly; there was no time to see even half the things on her list because she idled along one street after the other, each one looking more like something out of Grimm's Fairy Tales than the last; even the sight of the inhabitants in modern dress didn't quite disillusion her. She became hopelessly lost, which didn't matter at first until she glanced at her wrist-watch and knew that she was going to be late for tea. She was forced to show the name of the café Sieske had written down for her to the only person in sight, a short thick-set man coming towards her on the opposite side of the narrow cobbled street—he wore a semi-nautical cap and an oil-stained shirt, its buttons strained to bursting point across a powerful chest. She addressed him, absurdly, in English. 'Excuse me, but would you tell me how to find this café?'

She smiled at him and thrust the piece of paper under his nose. He read it very slowly, addressed her cheerfully, unintelligibly and at some length, and caught her arm in a massive paw. She trotted along beside him, having rather a job to keep up in her high heels and wondering if perhaps she had been a little foolish. Supposing he hadn't understood? She looked around and recognized nothing at all. They seemed to be going up and down a great many streets, each of them exactly like its fellows. She tugged his arm so that he stopped, showed him the paper again and felt relieved when he smiled hugely, showing some terrible teeth, and caught hold of her arm again, walking faster than ever. They turned a corner and she heard the hum of traffic and presently saw the main road before them. They came to a halt and he pointed to her left and smiled again. Harriet decided that he was rather nice and wished she could have thanked him in his own language. She managed a *Dank U* and remembered the packet of English cigarettes in her handbag. She pulled them out to offer him, then shook his hand because everyone shook hands in Holland and it seemed the polite thing to do. Before she turned the corner again she turned round and they waved to each other like old friends. The café was very close, she could see Sieske and Wierd looking rather anxiously in the opposite direction. Sieske turned round and saw her and said with her usual calm,

'There you are. We were wondering what had happened.'

Harriet told them as they sat over their tea, and they laughed a great deal and ate a number of cream cakes because they looked so delicious and Wierd was anxious that they should. Afterwards they walked slowly back to the car and on the way Harriet stopped to buy postcards so that Sieske and Wierd could say good-bye without her there to watch. By the time she had caught up with them they had reversed the car on to the road and she felt a secret relief that she hadn't been sitting in it; it would be so easy to accelerate into the canal instead of reversing. She got in and they went slowly down the street, waving to Wierd as they went, and then out of the town and on to the motorway. It was still quite early, just after five, and they were ahead of the great surge of traffic which would pour on to the roads after the day's work. They made good time, not stopping to dawdle and look at the view as they had done in the morning; they were half-way across the Afsluitdijk and it was almost eight o'clock when Harriet saw the AC 428 coming towards them, very fast. Not so fast, however, that she was plainly able to see Friso Eijsinck wave a careless gloved hand as they passed. The black-haired girl beside straight ahead of her and took no notice at all. Sieske said placidly, 'That was Friso.'

'Yes,' said Harriet in a calm voice which quite hid her own astonishment at the feelings their encounter had stirred up. 'What sort of fish do they catch in the Ijsselmeer?'

She had asked that question already on the way to Delft that morning. She was conscious of Sieske looking at her before she replied. 'Eels, mostly. Do you know who that girl was?'

'No,' said Harriet, 'and I'm not in the least interested.'

'No? Well, I suppose not. But you fit into everything so well here, I keep forgetting that you're not going to stay.' She slowed down to go through the outskirts of Harlingen. 'There's no reason why you should be interested in people you may never see again.'

Harriet swallowed and said carefully, 'No.' She felt like bursting into tears, which she told herself was very silly of her. Instead she said too brightly,

'It was fun today, but I like Friesland. Does Wierd know yet where he'll be working after you're married?'

It was a red herring which lasted until they reached home.

They were all sitting round the table eating the meal Mevrouw Van Minnen had made the rest of the family wait for, when the front door was opened and closed again with a thud followed by silence. Harriet dissected her chop with

all the care of a young surgeon performing his
first operation. Only one person shut the door
like that, and only one person, despite his size,
walked so lightly that it was impossible to hear
him. She had got her breath nicely under control
by the time the door opened and Friso walked
in. He returned a cheerful *Dag* to the chorus of
greetings, and added, presumably for her benefit,
'Hullo.'

She looked up briefly and said 'Hullo' before
returning to her chop, while Taeike jumped up
and made room for him at the table, and Maggina
ran to get a fresh plate and Mevrouw Van
Minnen made haste to serve him. He sat down
beside Taeike, ruffling her hair as he did so, and
accepted his supper with every sign of content.
Harriet passed him the pepper and salt and when
he asked, 'Did you have a good day in Delft?'
replied in a composed voice that yes, she had
enjoyed herself immensely.

'What did you see?' he wanted to know,
making short work of a chop. She told him, and
watched his eyebrows lift. 'Why,' he remarked,
'you didn't see the half!'

She would have been content to let it rest at
that, but Sieske told him laughingly that Harry
had gone off on her own and got herself lost,
and would have doubtless have missed her tea
altogether if it hadn't been for the good offices
of the man in the semi-nautical cap. Harriet sat

silently waiting for him to laugh, but instead he looked annoyed, and said in a critical tone which had the effect of infuriating her,

'You should know better than to wander off on your own like that.'

Her beautiful eyes shone very blue through the narrowed lids, but she said mildly enough, 'I'm not a child, Dr Eijsinck, and I have a tongue in my head!'

He shot an amused glance across the table. 'In many ways you are a child,' he observed, 'and you forget that the tongue in your head is a foreign one.'

She sat staring at him, longing to pick a quarrel, but with the Van Minnen family laughing and talking around them, it was impossible to do so, and he knew it. Instead she said with false meekness,

'I daresay it was very stupid of me—I fear my education was sadly lacking, for I can only speak my own language.'

'Now you have made me out to be a pompous ass,' he protested, amidst the general laughter—but not quite general, Harriet noted. Taeike frowned and protested too with a look of fury on her pretty face, and as soon as she could make herself heard, begged Friso to help her with her homework.

'But I'm tired out,' he said, looking exactly the reverse. 'I've not had a minute to myself

since Sunday luncheon.' He caught Harriet's eye
and grinned wickedly. 'You'll bear me out, will
you not, Harriet?'

She felt her cheeks grow warm. He had no
right to talk to her like that, just because she
had known who was lunching with him then,
and had seen him taking the girl home—presumably—more than twenty-four hours later. She
said in a quiet little voice, despite the tell-tale
cheeks,

'Why, certainly, Doctor Eijsinck. I'm sure you
have very little time to yourself, but I daresay
you like it like that. Though I can't say that you
look very tired.'

She didn't smile at him, but at Taeike instead,
who, however, didn't smile back. Harriet wondered why she was upset and then forgot about
it as Friso pushed back his chair and spoke
laughingly to Mevrouw Van Minnen, then pulled
Taeike to her feet. 'Ten minutes, and not a
second more,' he said as they went towards
the door.

He was back in the drawing-room, playing
chess with his partner long before Sieske and
Harriet had cleared the table and carried the supper dishes into the kitchen for the daily maid
to deal with in the morning. The two men sat,
wrapped in a companionable silence and a great
deal of smoke from their pipes while Mevrouw
Van Minnen sat at her pretty little rosewood

worktable, stitching at her gros-point. The two girls joined her and fell to discussing their plans for a trip to Amsterdam. There were relatives there, it would be easy to stay a night, even two. It was unthinkable that they should allow Harriet to go home without seeing something of the capital. There were the lesser but nevertheless interesting attractions of Leeuwarden to be sampled too, but Aede would take care of that, said Sieske; he planned to take Harry off for the day when next he was free.

She went away to fetch the coffee and presently returned with the tray; her return coincided with the chess game ending in stalemate, and the reappearance of Maggina and Taeike, very cheerful now that their homework was done. They sat around drinking the delicious coffee, arguing as to what Harriet should and should not see when she went to Amsterdam.

'And what does Harriet wish to see?' inquired Dr Eijsinck, who had said very little until that moment.

'Canals and old houses and flower stalls and one of those street organs,' she answered promptly, then added hastily for fear of decrying their kindness, 'and all the other things you have suggested as well.'

Dr Van Minnen laughed. 'At that rate, you will need to spend the rest of your holiday in Amsterdam, and that we cannot allow.'

Dr Eijsinck didn't get up to go until the two younger girls had gone up to bed.

'Will you all come over tomorrow evening?' He looked at Mevrouw Van Minnen and then turned to his partner. 'Any calls can be put through for you.' He had spoken in Dutch and was answered in that language before he turned to Harriet and said with casual friendliness,

'Everyone is coming over to my place tomorrow evening for dinner—naturally you are included in the invitation, Harriet.'

She thanked him politely, surprised to glimpse a look on his face which belied the formality of the words. She was even more taken aback when he added, 'Have you done any sailing, Harriet? I'm free after midday tomorrow; I wondered if you would like to come on the Sneekermeer— I've a boat there.'

She felt her heart race, which was absurd. . . he doubtless wanted a crew, and there was no one else available. 'What sort of boat?' she asked cautiously.

He looked surprised. 'A Sturgeon.' He had answered readily enough; probably he thought she had asked out of politeness. She forbore to mention that her three brothers, when not engrossed in cars, found solace in boats and when there had been no one else around, she had crewed.

'I'd like that very much,' she said finally.

He nodded briefly. 'Good, I'll fetch you about half past one. Wear something sensible and warm; you can bring a dress and change at my place.' He nodded again, and a minute later she heard the gentle roar of his car.

She didn't sleep very well, thinking about him. She had already realized that she was becoming obsessed by Friso Eijsinck; if she wasn't careful, she would lose her head over him completely, and what, she asked herself bitterly, could be sillier or more useless than that? The knowledge that she was past preventing this sorry state of affairs anyway added to her misery. She lay forlorn in bed and didn't bother to wipe away the tears trickling down her cheeks. They were still wet when she finally went to sleep.

He came for her at half past one the following day. She had done as she had been told and as well as slacks and a sweater had borrowed a pullover of Sieske's—its polo neck hugged her ears and the sleeves had to be rolled up, but it would be warm. She had borrowed a pair of the right sort of shoes from Maggina, too. Her hair hung in a shining plait over one shoulder and she hadn't bothered with make-up, only lipstick. Experience had taught her that men who ask girls to crew don't particularly mind what they look like, as long as they can handle a tiller and don't fall overboard. She went out to the car, a silk jersey dress over one arm, and a pair of shoes and a handbag in her hand. Dr Eijsinck, looking, if that were possible, larger than ever in an Aran sweater, took them from her and put them in the back of the car and said with faint surprise, 'Is this all you have with you?'

It was Harriet's turn to look surprised. 'Should I have brought something else?' she inquired.

He opened the door of the car for her to get in. 'Hairpins and things,' he hazarded.

'In my bag. My hair comes down if there's much wind, and then it's a nuisance.'

He had settled himself beside her and started the car. 'So you have sailed before.'

She glanced sideways at him and he returned her look with a bland one of his own. She said with a little air of apology, 'I've sailed with my brothers during the holidays. Dinghies mostly, and only when there wasn't anyone else around who could do it better.'

He laughed. 'Your opinion of yourself is a low one, Harry, yet I imagine that you do most things well.'

They had left the town behind, and were making their way across country towards Sneek. He drove fast but never carelessly and she supposed that he would handle a boat in the same efficient way. She felt absurdly elated by his compliment, although upon reflection it was the sort of remark that one could safely make to a schoolteacher or someone similar. . .but of course, she was something similar. Nurses and teachers did the same work, the one for the mind, the other for the body. Her spirits, which had begun to rise a little after her bad night, sank to new depths. He said with disconcerting perception, 'I didn't mean to make you sound like an elderly schoolteacher.'

She smiled ruefully. 'All the same, I'm a not so young nurse—that's much the same sort of thing.'

'How old are you?' he asked.

'Twenty-four.'

'With a successful career before you, so I hear. Surely it would suit you better to marry?'

The question was thrown at her carelessly; he sounded like the head of the family giving a poor relation some good advice. She lost her temper. 'Only if I can marry for money,' she said in a tight little voice. 'I don't care what the man's like just so long as I have a great many clothes and furs and jewels. . .' She stopped, appalled at the awful lies she was telling him. Her flash of temper had gone.

He said in a shocked voice, 'That's not true, I simply don't believe you.' He pulled the car into the side of the road and turned to look at her. 'Well?' he asked.

She felt her face redden, but said at once, 'Of course it wasn't true. You made me angry.' She didn't explain why. 'I don't care tuppence if my husband has any money or not. I don't think money is the most important thing in life. . .' Her face flamed anew. 'I'm sorry,' she said awkwardly, 'I forgot. Sieske said you were very rich. I didn't mean to be rude.'

He laughed with genuine amusement. 'Yes, I am, and although it's nice to have most of the things I want, I agree with you, money isn't important. I should be quite happy without it.'

She smiled. 'Oh, yes, I know. At least I. . .' she faltered, 'I think you are that kind of person.'

He started the car again. 'As I said before, Harriet, you aren't like anybody else.'

He flashed her a smile of such tenderness that her breath forsook her and by the time she had regained it they were approaching the outskirts of Sneek and she was able to plunge into a great many questions about the town, all of which he answered with great patience, not looking at her, so that she was unable to see the laughter in his eyes. But they held no mockery, only the lingering tenderness.

The boat was a beauty. Harriet inspected her with the thoroughness that was part of her nature, and when he asked her, half laughing, if she approved of it, said seriously,

'She's beautiful. I hope I shall do all the right things.'

He laughed, tossed her a yellow inflatable waistcoat and said,

'Put that on for a start, in case I throw you overboard in a fit of rage.'

She did as she was told. 'Do you have rages?' she asked.

He was busy with the sail and looked at her over his shoulder.

'Occasionally,' he conceded, 'but don't worry, I don't feel one coming on today.' He was smiling, and she smiled too, feeling suddenly happy. The sky was blue, filling slowly with little puffs of cloud; the boat danced gently under her feet. Why was it, she wondered, that being in a boat was like being in another world?

They went down the waterway to the lake with the wind behind them and set course for the opposite shore, sitting side by side in the cockpit with Harriet at the tiller. There were perhaps half a dozen boats sharing the Sneekermeer with them, and none of those near. They talked about boats and gardens and inevitably, hospital, and then boats again.

'I love those big curved boats with prows,' said Harriet, pointing to one.

'A *botter*,' he explained. 'I've got one—it's in the boatyard being repainted. I don't go out in her often though, only when there are half a dozen of us—it's a family boat; very safe, and ideal for children. When I marry I shall pack my entire family on board and sail away for several weeks at a time.'

She looked away from him and said in a quiet voice, 'That sounds nice,' and then, to change the subject, 'Are they seaworthy?'

She got to know quite a lot about him that afternoon. He was not a man to talk much about himself, but by the time they turned for home she had a pretty good idea of his background and likes and dislikes. And she, hardly realizing it, had talked too—about her family and her work and the elderly pony she still rode when she went home. They didn't talk so much on the way back, for there was more to do and it took longer too; tacking into the wind. They could have used the engine, but Friso told her that he only used it to take the boat in and out or if he was pressed for time. The sky had clouded over; the small clouds that had looked so harmless an hour or so earlier had joined themselves together, swallowing the blue above them. The wind had freshened too, but Harriet wasn't cold; her cheeks were gloriously pink, and her eyes shone, and although the wind had ruffled her hair, the thick plait still lay neatly over her shoulder. She looked round once to find Friso staring at her, his grey eyes brilliant. She put a hand up to her hair and asked,

'Is there something the matter?'

His eyes held hers. 'No,' he said, his deep

voice suddenly harsh. 'You're beautiful, Harriet. You must have been told that many times before.'

When she didn't answer, he went on sharply, 'You do know you're beautiful?'

Harriet turned from the contemplation of a pair of swans flying with swift grace towards the reeds at the lake edge.

'Yes,' she said composedly. 'I should be stupid if I didn't—just as you would be stupid or a hypocrite if you didn't admit to your own good looks. But you're neither, and I don't suppose you give it a thought. Well, neither do I.' She grinned like a little girl. 'You should see my sisters; they're really beautiful.'

He chuckled. 'You disarm me, Harriet. Tell me about them.'

'They're married; Diana has three boys; Rosemary has a girl and a boy.'

He trimmed the sail. 'Older than you?'

'Oh yes. I'm in the middle—my brothers are younger than I.'

She altered course a little in obedience to his nod. 'I was to have been a boy. Henry after my grandfather. . .'

'Ah, now I know why you're called Harry. It couldn't be a more unsuitable name. You are. . . very much a girl.'

His steady gaze met hers across the boat. It needed a great effort to look away from him and a still greater effort to control her breath. She swallowed back the wave of excitement which threatened to engulf her and said the first thing which came into her head.

'I suppose you are much older than your. . .' she stopped. 'I mean, are you the eldest?' She had gone a little pink and went pinker when he laughed and said, 'Yes, but I'm not as elderly as your tone implies, although I'm ten years older than you.' He added outrageously to make her gasp, 'I prefer my girl-friends to be at least ten years younger than myself.'

She said, 'But I'm. . .' and stopped herself just in time. If she should disclaim any desire to be one of his girl-friends he was quite capable of agreeing with her most readily. After all, she wasn't; at least. . . Instead she said, 'There's a great deal of cloud. Do you suppose it will rain before we get back?'

His smile was gently mocking. 'Ah, the weather. Such a safe subject,' and proceeded to sustain a conversation on the subject which lasted, on and off, until he brought the car to a standsill outside his house door. His knowledge of the elements, in their every aspect, appeared to be a profound one; Harriet's ears buzzed with facts about cumuli, low pressure and humidity. She had answered suitably when comment had been called for, because she was by nature a nicely mannered girl, but as she got out of the car she gave him a speaking glance and then almost choked when he said silkily, 'It was you who wanted to talk about the weather, Harriet.'

He walked round the car to where she was standing and threw a massive arm around her shoulders. She stood very still under it, her heart thumping, and was conscious of deep disappointment when all he did was to urge her forward, up the steps to where Wim was waiting at the open door. Inside, he released her, saying merely,

'Letje will take you upstairs. You'll want to change. The others will be here in half an hour or so.'

She left him standing in the hall and followed the soft-footed, smiling Letje up the stairs; at least she was going to see something of the house.

CHAPTER SIX

THE room she was ushered into was at the side of
the house, overlooking the path she had walked
along with Friso. She stood at the window looking down at it and sighed without knowing it
before turning away to study her surroundings.
They were charming. The room was, by her own
standards, large, and furnished in the Empire
period—the bed, dressing-table and wardrobe
were mahogany and vast; they shared a patina
of well-cared-for age. In any other, smaller room
they might have been overpowering, but here
they were exactly right; set off by a skilful scat-
tering of small satin-covered chairs with
buttoned backs and elaborately pleated skirts.
There was a satinwood writing table under the
window and a work-table in Japanese lacquer,
very small and dainty. A little round table with
piecrust edge stood companionably by one of
the chairs, bearing a bowl of spring flowers;
they smelled with a faint fragrance and made the
room seem lived in, although she guessed that
it was seldom used. There were portraits on the
walls too—rather austere gentlemen in wigs or
high cravats, according to their period; their

wives—presumably their wives—looked soberly down at Harriet from heavy frames, their
dim rich silks setting off the magnificence of
their meticulously painted jewels. She thought
she detected a fleeting resemblance to Friso in
some of the faces; he had certainly inherited their
austerity of looks upon occasion. She realized all
at once that she had been wasting time and went
into the adjoining bathroom and turned on the
taps. She would have to hurry.

She was putting on her lipstick when there
was a tap on the door and Sieske came in.

'Harry, did you have a good time?' She eyed
her friend critically. 'How nice you look—that's
a lovely dress.' She went and sat on one of the
little chairs and Harriet put away the lipstick and
looked down at herself.

It was a pretty dress; a soft gold-coloured
sheath, patterned with honeysuckle; she had felt
rather guilty when she had bought it, for it had
cost a lot of money; now her feeling was one of
satisfaction. Without doubt it did something for
her. She hoped that Friso would share her
opinion.

It seemed he did not, for beyond a laughing
reference to her seamanship as he offered a glass
of sherry, he addressed her in only the most
general of terms throughout the evening. The
oyster soup, the fillets of sole Maconaise, the
saddle of lamb—even the sweet—some frothy

confection of marrons glacés—Anna's own invention—were dust in her pretty mouth.

She allowed none of her true feelings to show, however, and laughed and talked with the faintly shy air which she had never managed to overcome. Whenever the opportunity presented itself, she surveyed her surroundings. The dining-room was large and square and in the front of the house; its walls were panelled with a wood she couldn't identify; it was furnished with the massive round table at which they sat. It had been made to accommodate a dozen guests at the least, but now the ribbon-back chairs had been reduced to a paltry seven. The sideboard, large and splendidly simple, took up most of one wall, and all around them were more portraits of bygone Eijsincks, their painted eyes watching each morsel of food she ate. She looked away from a particularly haughty old gentleman with sidewhiskers and encountered Friso's lifted brows. He looked so like the portrait that she averted her gaze and applied herself to her dinner.

They sat after dinner in the salon, drinking their coffee and something richly potent and velvety from delicate liqueur glasses. Harriet, sharing one of the sofas with Maggina, was content to listen, for the most part, to the conversation around her—the easy, not too serious talk of old friends. She longed to explore the room thoroughly, to pick up the china pieces lying about and examine them and run her hand down the thick velvet folds of the curtains. Everything was so very beautiful. She checked a sigh, looked up and caught Friso's eye upon her again.

It was soon after this that the front door knocker suddenly reverberated through the house, not once, but half a dozen times, to cease as suddenly, presumably upon the opening of the door. Everyone had stopped talking to listen to the faint agitated voice from the hall, and every head turned as Wim came in, moving somewhat faster than was his wont, and bent to speak quietly in his master's ear. He had barely finished what he was saying before the doctor was on his feet. He said something in his turn to Dr Van Minnen in a crisp voice totally unlike his usual slight drawl, so that gentleman got to his feet and started for the door. Harriet, seething with curiosity, was forced to sit quiet while he spoke to Mevrouw Van Minnen too. It wasn't until he was on the point of leaving them that he spoke to Sieske. He sounded like a general giving orders and he didn't wait to see if they had been understood. The two younger girls he ignored.

Sieske got to her feet and started to follow him from the room, saying over her shoulder, 'Come on, Harry. There's a car in the canal— they don't know yet who's in it—they'll bring

them here. We have to get the surgery ready.'
She led the way across the hall and opened a
door under the staircase and switched on the
light. Harriet, close on her heels, saw that the
surgery was roomy, with a door at the other end
of it, presumably leading to a side entrance. She
went straight across the room and opened the
door and found a light switch there too, which
shone on to the drive running alongside the
house. She had no idea how much time they
had; Sieske, who knew her way around, was
busy with the oxygen cylinder, fitting on the
tube and mask and putting the catheters ready.
Harriet began to clear what furniture there was
away from the centre of the room; they would
want all the space they could have if they had
to do any recussitation. She found a notepad and
pen, and several pairs of scissors which she took
from the well stocked instrument cabinet in one
corner. There were some syringes and needles
there too; she took those as well and cleared a
space on the doctor's desk and arranged them
neatly where they could be got at in a hurry.
She wasn't sure that the doctor would approve
of the way she had piled his papers and swept
them to one side. In her experience, doctors in
general practice preferred to work at a desk clut-
tered with unread circulars, cryptic notes on the
backs of envelopes, electricity bills, samples of
pills, snapshots of their loved ones and a great

variety of official forms. It seemed to her that Friso's desk ran true to form. She said without turning round,

'Has anyone telephoned the police and the ambulance?'

'Wim,' replied Sieske. She had her head in a wall cupboard. 'There's plenty of Savlon; I'll put some into a couple of gallipots and dilute enough to fill a jug. Someone's sure to need cleaning up.'

Harriet nodded to the back of her friend's head, 'Blankets?' she asked.

'Wim,' said Sieske, emerging. Harriet flew across the hall in search of him, encountered him coming through a door beyond the stairs and remembered too late that she didn't know the word for blankets. She stopped before him and said hopelessly, 'Blankets, Wim.' And he said, 'Yes, miss, I have them here.' He indicated a pile of them beyond the door and began to pile them into her arms; when he thought she had enough he said, 'I'll bring the rest, miss.' She went back across the hall, thinking that it was just like Friso to have a servant who spoke English when required. It was quite good English too.

She piled the blankets neatly on to the doctor's chair, and Wim went away again, presumably to fetch more. There were sounds of feet coming along the drive and a moment later Dr Van

Minnen and another man came in carrying a man
between them; he streamed water, his clothes
plastered with mud and weed; his face was
white, his eyes closed. They put him carefully
on the floor and Dr Van Minnen dropped down
on his knees beside him while his helper
squelched his way out again. Sieske was already
on the other side of the prone figure, but Harriet
wasted no time in watching her, for Friso had
come in through the door carrying an elderly
woman. He laid her down with the same care
as the others had used and Harriet rolled the
unconscious form expertly over into the prone
position, turned the limp head gently to one side
and swept a hand into the mouth, but the
woman's teeth were her own; there was no
danger there. She swept the sopping arms above
her patient's head, and then sank back on her
heels and put her hands on the small of the
woman's back.

'I see you know what you're about,' said Friso
from above her, and was gone. It was hard work,
but worth it; for after a few minutes she felt the
first faint movement in the body beneath her
hands; she persevered and was rewarded by the
faint tinge of colour in the white cheeks, before
long she saw the slight fluttering of the woman's
eyelids. She stopped her efforts long enough to
catch at a still flaccid wrist and check the pulse;
it was weak but steady. Harriet straightened her

back and found ... by her, holding ... uw Van Minnen standing woman in it between ...et. They wrapped the her wet clothing, beginn ...nd began to remove Harriet had barely unlaced ...ith her shoes. But there was a commotion at the ... of them when Friso came in with a half-grown bo ... again and one brief glance in Harriet's direction an ... said, 'Leave the woman to Mevrouw Van Minnen and come here. I've emptied his lungs.'

He laid the boy down and Harriet saw at once that they wouldn't be able to turn him over because of the wound in his chest. It wasn't a large wound, but a circular depression, oozing with a gentle persistence. Someone had opened his jacket and shirt, probably to see where he was hurt. She snatched up a wad of gauze and covered it, then took another piece of gauze and opened the boy's mouth to catch and hold his tongue. Friso had peeled off his jacket and she saw that he was soaked and as muddy as the boy he had brought in. He knelt down behind the boy's head, caught his arms above the elbow and started artificial respiration. It wasn't an ideal state of affairs, for the chest wound needed urgent attention, but still more urgent was the task of getting the boy to breathe again.

'Let go his tongue,' said Friso, and started the kiss of life. Released, Harriet got to her feet and started to collect swabs and dressings; there

TEMPESTUOUInus injection too,
would have to be an ~grene. She went back
as well as one for g~ctor what she had done,
to the boy, told th~them both now?' and at his
asked, 'Shall L~erself of scissors and began to
nod, possess~
cut the w~ ~leeve open.

It ~~s wonderful when the boy started
to br~athe—he was shocked and severely
injured—it was hard to know just how severely
until he could be got to hospital, but at least he
was alive; all three of them were alive. She got
the oxygen and fixed it up and set about cleaning
the wound. She had just about finished when a
great many people arrived at once—the police,
who came in quietly and got busy with note-
books and quiet questions, and the ambulance
men with their stretchers. The man and woman
were conscious now and able to answer the few
essential questions which were put to them, the
boy lay quiet, his breath fluttering, his face
bluish-white. Dr Eijsinck, using a sharper tone
than Harriet had ever heard before, but not rais-
ing his voice at all, said something—sufficient
to cause the boy to be lifted carefully on to a
stretcher and borne away without further ado.
She heard the ambulance a moment later, its
sing-song warning sounding loud on the night
air, moving fast along the road. His mother and
father followed him a few minutes later, leaving
the rest of them standing in a welter of discarded

blankets, stray fragments of wet clothing, used
swabs and a good deal of weed and mud. Wim,
who, Harriet suspected, had been doing a great
deal in an unobtrusive way, was already col-
lecting blankets, but when Dr Eijsinck said,
'Coffee, I think, Wim,' he relinquished the task
to Mevrouw Van Minnen and went away. Sieske
had her head in the cupboard again, putting back
what she had taken out. Harriet turned to the
desk and began to clear away the small paraphernalia—swabs, scissors, gallipots—she cleaned
them all in turn and returned them where they
belonged, then returned to restore the desk to its
original state of ordered chaos. She had picked
up an old copy of the *Lancet* and was trying to
remember if it had been under the blotter or with
a pile of circulars she had swept aside, when
Friso, who was conferring with Dr Van Minnen
and the policemen, broke off the conversation
long enough to say, mildly,

'Don't bother, Harry. My desk needed a
clean-up anyway.'

She put the *Lancet* down thankfully and went
to fold blankets with Mevrouw Van Minnen—
they had them tidy just as Wim came back and
informed them, in two languages, that coffee
was in the salon, and the two young ladies were
anxious for news. 'The gentlemen,' he added,
'will take their coffee where they are.'

Maggina and Taeike fell upon them when they

reached the salon, slightly aggrieved that they
had not been allowed to help but nevertheless
curious to hear what had occurred. The three
ladies spent a pleasurable half hour answering
their questions, repairing their make-up and
drinking a great many cups of coffee, and deplor-
ing the muddy state of their shoes and stockings.
Harriet glanced down at her own dress and saw
the little blobs of dried mud and pieces of weed
and here and there, small specks of blood. The
dress, she thought regretfully, would never be
quite the same again. The two doctors came in
presently—the police had gone and the men had
changed into dry clothes, Dr Van Minnen rather
precariously rigged out in a shirt and trousers of
Friso's. He lowered his rather portly frame into
a chair, remarking that he must have put on
weight for everything was so tight. His homely
little joke relieved a little of the delayed excitement and tension and when Wim appeared with
a tray on which was a tall silver jug and some
glasses the atmosphere lightened considerably.
Harriet took a sip of the frothy yellow liquid,
and found it to be warm. It was only after she had
swallowed that she discovered it to be extremely
fiery as well. She choked a little, and Friso, who
had sat down opposite her, raised an eyebrow
at her and asked, 'Do you like it, Harriet? It's
Cambridge Punch, from a very old English
recipe, and a splendid pick-me-up.'

She took another cautious sip; it really was very nice. 'What's in it?' she asked.

'Eggs, milk, brandy and rum.' He smiled suddenly and kindly at her. 'Just what you need after all that excitement. You worked like a beaver; thank you, Harry.'

There was really nothing she could say—'Not at all' would sound ridiculous—so would 'It was a pleasure.' She smiled shyly and took another sip and felt the rum and brandy combine to give her a pleasant glow inside.

Everyone was suddenly talking at once again, and he didn't speak to her again. It was only when they were on the point of leaving that he asked her, 'Do you like my home, Harriet?'

He had her hand between his own and showed no sign of relinquishing it. She looked up at him. 'Yes, Friso, very much.'

'As I had hoped,' was all he said. She fell asleep that night still wondering what exactly he had meant.

CHAPTER SEVEN

AEDE telephoned the next morning; he would be free on the following day, he explained, so how would Harriet like to spend it with him in Leeuwarden. She agreed readily, suppressing the thought that if she did so, she would be unable to see Friso, always supposing that he came to his partner's house. She thanked Aede with a false enthusiasm and went to find Sieske.

When she awoke the next day, it was to find the sky shrouded in high grey cloud, and by the time Aede arrived to fetch her, another lower layer of cloud was scudding in from the sea, blown by a wind which whined and whistled around the housetops. The road to Leeuwarden looked bare and sad; the country on either side unprotected.

'It's very flat,' said Harriet. 'The sea could rush in.'

Aede laughed comfortably. 'You forget our dykes; they do not break so easily—it would need an earthquake or a bomb; besides, there are always men watching.'

It was a comforting thought; Harriet turned her attention to the city outskirts, and forgot the weather. They were driving down a rather dull road which led to a roundabout surrounded by modern buildings, then suddenly they were in the old city—there was nothing dull about the canal they crossed to enter the bustling, shop-lined street, bisected by a much bridged canal. The shops were modern, but above them rose a variety of old roofs, which Harriet found enchanting, but when she begged Aede to stop, he said,

'Lord, no. Not here. We'll go and have coffee and leave the car at the hotel; then we can walk around.'

At the end of the street, past the old Weigh House, he turned into an even busier street, crossed the canal again and stopped outside a pleasant hotel overlooking a square. They got out, and before they went inside. Aede took her arm and turned her round.

'This is our most important statue,' he explained, and pointed towards a pedestal upon which stood a cow. 'Our prosperity.' he said simply. 'We owe it to our cows.'

They drank their coffee in the hotel, sitting in the window of the café overlooking the busy square, talking leisurely about the happenings of the previous week.

'Did you enjoy Delft?' Aede asked.

Harriet nibbled the little sugary biscuit which had come with her coffee. 'Very much—I got

lost.' She told him all about it and he laughed
and then said, 'But you should be careful, you
know, you're a foreigner—you must never go
off on your own again.'

'That's what Friso said.'

'Did he? Well, yes, naturally.' He stopped
abruptly, and Harriet knitted her brows, trying
to make sense of this remark. Why should it be
natural for Friso to be concerned about her? She
pondered it briefly and then went faintly pink
as a possible solution struck her, to be at once
cast down by Aede's next words.

'What I meant was, Friso would have said
that to any pretty girl.' He frowned, hunting for
words. Harriet achieved a creditable smile.

'Aede, what a nice compliment! And now do
tell me what we're going to do first.'

He responded to this conversational red herring with an obvious relief.

'How about the Museum—the Friesian
Museum? We could walk there and pick the car
up later.'

They set off, back over the canal, driven to
walk at a furious pace by the ferocious wind.
The sky seemed lower and blacker than ever, but
at least it wouldn't rain until the wind died down.

They walked along arm in arm, talking
comfortably. 'Where's your hospital?' asked
Harriet.

Aede waved a careless arm. 'Over there. Just

outside the town. It's new, not completed, in fact, but there's plenty of work just the same.'

He went on talking about it until they reached the museum, which had once upon a time been a private mansion and still contrived to look like one. The curator was large and white-haired and spoke scholarly English in a gentle voice. Harriet thought that Friso would look something like him in twenty years or so. The train of thought set up by this idea was broken only by Aede's quite dramatic description of Great Pier's achievements in the sixteenth century. Judging by the size of the sword she was called upon to examine this Friesian hero must have been a giant even amongst his own giant-like race. They stayed a long time, going from room to room; sometimes the curator joined them for a few minutes, but most of the time Aede painstakingly led her round; he seemed to be enjoying it as much as she. It was almost two o'clock when they got back to the hotel for lunch, and the wind showed no signs of abating. Now there were short flurries of rain—they decided to stay in Leeuwarden for the rest of the day, and in spite of the worsening weather, they prowled happily up and down the narrow lanes, looking at the old, small houses, while Aede pointed out their architectural points, and when Harriet at length had had her fill, they strolled in and out of the shops, where she bought presents to take home—silver teaspoons and Makkum pottery, and tobacco for her father. They had forgotten all about tea and presently they went back to the hotel again and sat over drinks and then ate a leisurely meal before going back to Franeker. The countryside looked even more desolate in the heavy dusk; the road stretched before them, shining wetly. Harriet was glad when they stopped outside the cheerfully lighted house in Franeker. It was pleasant to sit quietly, talking about their day with the rest of the family, and drinking Mevrouw Van Minnen's excellent coffee. The howling wind and rain beating on the windows seemed curiously unreal heard from the comfort of the sitting-room. Aede got reluctantly to his feet after a time and went off, cheerfully enough, back to his hospital in Leeuwarden. After he'd gone, the rest of them sat around, still talking.

'Friso's on call,' remarked Doctor Van Minnen. 'I hope he won't need to go out tonight.'

Harriet remembered his remark when she was lying in bed, listening to the storm. She wondered if anyone bothered to see that Friso had a hot drink and took off his wet clothes when he went out on a bad night. She worried about it for quite a time until her common sense told her that he had servants enough to look after him. He didn't look in the least neglected. She turned over, thumping her pillow with an unnecessary violence, and told herself that she was a fool, and after a little while went to sleep.

She awoke the next morning to a sudden fierce clap of thunder. The wind had apparently gathered strength from the night hours; so had the rain. She turned from the unpleasing prospect outside as Sieske tapped on the door and came in. She was already dressed and offered the information that she would have to go to Sneek after breakfast. Oma wasn't well—she would have to take the Mini and see what was the matter.

'I'll not ask you to come with me, Harry,' she said. 'Not in this weather. Father has gone to Leeuwarden—he's anaesthetizing at the hospital today. Do you mind being at home with Moeder?'

'Me?' asked Harriet. 'No, of course not. I shall air my Dutch.' She was putting up her hair and her mouth was full of pins; she said indistinctly, 'Isn't there a surgery here today?'

Sieske uncurled herself from the bed. 'No. Friso sees Father's urgent cases when he's at the hospital; but he doesn't come here.' She didn't look at Harriet. 'He just does the visits.' Harriet didn't speak, so after a minute she went on, 'I've been listening to the news—the wind's done quite a lot of damage and there's a little flooding locally—It's the spring tide, you know, and the wind blowing from the north-west at the same time.'

They went downstairs to breakfast.

The morning passed slowly; Harriet and Mevrouw Van Minnen had an early lunch—there wasn't much else to do and it kept their minds off the dismal scene outside. Sieske had telephoned from Sneek, and although she had made light of it, they gathered that she had had a very unpleasant journey. It was shortly after that the telephone went dead. They were in the sitting-room, improving Harriet's Dutch when they heard a car coming wetly along the street. It stopped; brakes squealing, outside the house, and Mevrouw Van Minnen, who had gone to look out of the window, said, '*De jeep van Friso*,' which remark Harriet was well able to understand. She got up and went to the window too. Why had Friso come? But it wasn't Friso who got out and ran up the steps to peal the bell with a desperate urgency, but a young man who was a stranger. He stood in the hall, dripping over the carpet, talking to Mevrouw Van Minnen. He spoke as though he was repeating a lesson learned by heart, and when he had finished, she nodded calmly and stood thinking. At length she turned to Harriet.

'Friso calls help. Calls for Sieske—baby.' She paused, frowning in deep concentration. Harriet snatched up her writing pad and pen and held

them out. Mevrouw Van Minnen nodded and
smiled and proceeded to draw a pair of forceps.
Harriet had no difficulty in recognizing them;
so Friso wanted to do a forceps delivery—he'd
want the Minnett's gas-air portable; she had seen
it in Doctor Van Minnen's surgery. Not to be
outdone by Mevrouw Van Minnen's basic
English, she said, '*Ik ga*.' She turned to go to
the surgery—she knew exactly what she would
need to take with her—but Mevrouw Van
Minnen put a hand on her arm and said painstakingly,

'Dyke break. Much water.' She held a hand
a foot or so above the floor, and looked hopefully
at Harriet, who made a frustrated sound which
changed to a crow of triumph as she remembered
the dictionary on the sitting-room table. With its
invaluable help and some lucky guesswork, she
possessed herself of the fact that there had been
some sort of accident to the sea dyke above the
patient's house; a small area was under water.
She would have liked to know more, but there
simply wasn't time—Friso was waiting.

She was ready in ten minutes. She had put on
slacks and a sweater and borrowed an anorak
and boots from Taeike's wardrobe. The needed
equipment stood in the hall while the messenger
swallowed coffee; he had said very little after
his one long speech, now he muttered something
to Mevrouw Van Minnen, shouldered the

Minnett's and opened the door. The Land-Rover seemed a haven of refuge after the few seconds' walk from the house. Harriet sighed soundlessly with relief and hoped that the journey was to be a short one. In this she was disappointed. Once out of the little town, they headed, as she knew they would, for the coast. It was slow progress in the teeth of the gale and the rain lashing down to flood the windscreen as though there were no wipers working, but in time they reached Tzummarum, which straddled the coast road. Harriet looked hopefully at her companion, and above the wind he shouted something at her and shook his head. Clearly, they had further to go.

It was at St Annaparochie, several kilometres further, that he turned off the road, and into a country lane winding past the church, straight to the sea. Perhaps in good weather it had a passable surface, but now it was covered in a wet sand which had turned to mud. Clear of the village, Harriet could see the flooded *polder* land with the sea dyke behind it. Her companion waved a vague arm towards the sea and, for the first time, smiled at her. She concluded that they were almost at the end of their journey, and sure enough, after a further five minutes of skidding and sliding in the mud, he drew up.

Harriet couldn't see anything at all when she first got out. The wind took her breath and the rain lashed her face with such frenzy that she was half blinded. She held on to the Land-Rover with all her might, and presently was able to take stock of her surroundings. The dyke was closer now; it looked undamaged, but in the distance, where it followed the curve of the coast, she could make out a great many figures moving what looked like a dragline; there was a pile of what might have been wreckage, but it was too far off to see. She transferred her gaze to the cottage under the dyke—it was already under water as far as its low window-sills, as was the larger house only a few hundred yards away from where they had stopped. She became aware that the man was beside her, and without a word, she picked up one of the bags and started down the small slippery path behind him. It led them to what she supposed was a field when it was dry; it was now boot-high in water, and was obviously going to get deeper as they proceeded. She sloshed along in her companion's wake, her thoughts intent on keeping her feet at all costs.

It was when they were level with the first house that she stopped. She had heard a faint whine, but when it wasn't repeated, she supposed that it was the wind, but after a few more steps she stopped again. The wind was whining; but this wasn't the wind. In the little yard behind the house there was a large ruffiany dog, up to his belly in water, and fastened securely to the wall by a stout rope. The man had gone past it with barely a glance; Harriet guessed that he was too worried about his wife to think of anything else; she would get no help from him, nor would he stop. It would only take a minute. She put her hand into the pocket of her slacks and withdrew the sort of all-purpose knife that all boys carry. It seemed a surprising thing for the delicate-looking and ultra-feminine Miss Slocombe to have about her person, but as she had once sensibly observed, it was only common sense to be equipped for any eventuality. She put the bag she was carrying on the top of a convenient wall and went over to the dog, selecting the strongest blade as she did so.

The man didn't look round until they were at the door of the cottage. Harriet stood quietly while he gave vent to his feelings. She gathered they weren't happy ones, and when he made to wade back towards the dog beside her, she put a protective hand on the shabby head pressed against her knee, and said, 'No. He stays here with me. I'll not leave him to drown.' She spoke with an air of authority which he could understand, even though her words were unintelligible. She walked past him, her hand on the beast's head and, still muttering, he pushed the door open and they went inside. The passage was small, with a door on either side and a narrow steep stair between; the water was already lapping the lower steps. They stood, the three of them, listening to the ceiling creaking under Dr Eijsinck's tread. He called out something as he came, and in a moment his long legs, encased in gumboots, appeared on the stairs. He stopped just above the water, staring at them. After a long silence he said in a cold voice to make her shiver,

'You! Why in heaven's name have you come here? I asked for Sieske. . .even if she couldn't come, surely someone could have been found.'

He looked so fierce that Harriet clutched the dog's fur harder and it whimpered softly. She said 'Sorry' and patted its dirty head. It gave her a moment to bottle up her rage, when she spoke her voice was as quiet and level as usual.

'Sieske's in Sneek. There's only her mother at home—and me. There was no time to find anyone else.' She swallowed returning rage. 'May I remind you that I am a nurse?'

He didn't appear to hear her. His eyes were on the dog. It stared at him with its yellow eyes, red tongue hung between terrifying teeth. Dr Eijsinck laughed softly, and with genuine amusement.

'Do tell me, Harriet, why have you brought this dog with you?'

She explained and added, 'Please don't let that man turn him loose. He's cold and wet and hungry.'

He didn't answer her, but turned to the man

and said something and the man growled a reply. 'Come upstairs then, since you are here, and bring that damned great beast with you.'

Upstairs was an attic, one corner of which had been boarded up to form a bedroom. Harriet peeled off her soaking anorak, bade the dog sit down and not stir and started to unpack the bags with a practised hand. The patient was dozing fitfully—worn out, she supposed. Friso was washing his hands in the little tin basin on the chest which was pushed against one wall. Without turning round, he asked,

'You understand Minnett's?'

Harriet tied the tapes of the gown which she had had the forethought to include in one of the bags, and started to lay out the things Friso would need; they were each packed in sealed packets, ready for use. She was trying, unsuccessfully, to forget the look of anger on his face when he had seen her—he had looked at her quite differently when they had gone sailing, and later that evening too. . .she brushed the thought aside and answered his question in a civil voice which betrayed nothing of her real feelings.

'Yes, Doctor, I do know about Dutch rules. In England, provided the patient has been previously examined and pronounced fit by the doctor, the midwife may administer gas-and-air analgesia from a Minnett's apparatus without supervision. I am a midwife,' she added unnecessarily.

He had his back to her, and in any case, she didn't look up from loosening the packs so that he could withdraw their contents with a sterile hand. He spoke softly. 'My good girl, are you presuming to teach me the rules?'

Harriet took a very small blanket out of one of the bags and laid it handy, ready for the baby.

'Certainly not,' she said briskly. 'I merely wish to reassure you.'

She squeezed her small person past his bulk and went to the head of the bed; the patient was awake. Harriet took her hand and smiled and nodded at her, waiting patiently for Friso to explain to the woman what had to be done.

The baby was a boy. Harriet wrapped him in the blanket with all the care of a saleswoman wrapping a valuable parcel, and gave him to his tired, happy mother, whose pulse, she noted, was too rapid. She told Friso, wondering if he would snub her again when she told him that she had brought two vacolitres of five per cent saline with her. He made it easy by telling her that the woman would have to go to Leeuwarden as soon as she could be moved.

'She'll need a transfusion, and this is no place for her at the moment.'

Harriet agreed soberly and mentioned the vacolitres, suffering a mixture of relief and disappointment when all he said was,

'Good girl—let's have one up, shall we?'

It only took a few minutes, then Friso called something through the half-open door and the man came in, smiling and faintly uneasy at the sight of his wife. Harriet took off her gown, listening with half an ear to the unintelligible talk, until Friso said, 'Coffee outside. We'll leave them for a bit.'

The dog was sitting where she had left him in a corner of the attic. He whined gently and wagged a stumpy tail, and she went and sat down beside him on the floor, leaving Friso to fetch two mugs of coffee from a table which also held a small paraffin stove and a collection of pots and pans and crockery. There was a box too, full of food, doubtless swept in haste from a downstairs cupboard. Furniture had been stacked neatly along one wall of the attic. Harriet wondered about the carpets.

'Will they get compensation?' she asked, accepting her coffee. Friso put a pan of water down in front of the dog, who drank with pathetic gusto, then fetched two chairs and, as an afterthought, an end of bread from the table. They sat side by side, watching the animal dispose of the unappetizing meal with a relish highlighted by a display of awesome teeth and rolling eye.

'Yes, but not at once. Don't worry about that.

It'll be seen to. Drink your coffee, then we can give Mevrouw Bal a cup and get things cleared up.' He took his watch out of a pocket and put it back on his wrist. 'It's almost six; the tide will be high at half past seven—we shall have to stay here.' He got up and went to peer out of the small window set in the attic wall.

Harriet drank her coffee, reserving the last of it for the dog. He licked the bowl hopefully long after no drop remained, then edged nearer to her so that she could put an arm round his matted woolly shoulders. She addressed Friso's back. 'How long shall we be here?'

He shrugged broad shoulders. 'Most of the night at least, I should suppose. Once the tide's on the turn they can get on with repairing the breach. If the ambulance can get through as far as Bal brought the Land-Rover, it'll be easy enough. While we're making his wife comfortable, he must go back to St Annaparochie and get the police to contact the hospital—they'll send an ambulance as soon as it's possible.' He turned round to look at her. There was no sign of anger in his face now; she wasn't sure of his expression, but there was something in it which emboldened her to ask, 'Why were you angry when I came?'

He came and stood in front of her, very close, so that he appeared even taller and broader than he was. 'Why do you suppose?' His voice was dry.

'Well,' she said carefully, 'I suppose you were disappointed because it was I and you were afraid that I wouldn't be able to help you or understand the Minnett's or—or make myself useful. I know,' she added mournfully, 'that you haven't got much of an opinion of me.'

'I was not aware that I had even offered an opinion of you—if you must know, I find you an excellent nurse, a woman of great good sense, and a beautiful and utterly charming companion. My anger was the result of my fears for your well-being, my dear—my very dear Harriet.'

He walked away as he spoke and she heard him talking to the couple in the bedroom, and a moment later Mijnheer Bal came out and went downstairs, and Friso put his head round the door and asked her to bring his patient a cup of coffee. His voice sounded so ordinary that she fancied that she must have imagined all that he had just said. But there was no time to think about it—she did as she was bid, and then, while Friso made shift to pack away the equipment, she washed the mother and bathed the baby and set the little room to rights, and when there was nothing more to do, she went back into the attic, feeling shy. Friso apparently did not share her feelings, for all he said was,

'Finished? Can you open a few tins and

warm something up for all of us to eat?'

Her practical nature took over, giving the shyness no chance. She said, 'Yes, of course,' and went to inspect the untidy pile of odds and ends on the table. From these she selected a number of tins and was pouring their contents into an iron pan she had providentially found in the clothes basket when Friso said, 'Need any help?' and strolled over to stand beside her. He eyed the neatly opened tins. 'Naturally, you carry a tin opener with you,' he murmured blandly. 'I should have known.'

Harriet looked apologetic. 'Well, not always, but I've a knife I usually carry around.'

'Ah, yes. With a corkscrew and that small instrument for digging stones out of horses' hooves.' His voice was grave, but he was laughing at her, though she didn't dare to look up and see. She said 'Yes,' rather shortly, and then, 'You're in my way. And we're running short of water.'

He picked up a kettle and a bucket and went obediently down the stairs. She could hear him wading about down below, and presently he began to whistle; the small domestic sound made everything very normal; she salted her pot-au-feu, unable to see it through sudden tears. She put down her spoon and brushed them away angrily, not sure why she was crying.

It was more than an hour before Bal returned;

by then the contents of the pot were giving off
a delicious aroma. Harriet had given Mevrouw
Bal her supper and tucked her up once more
with the baby and had then turned her attention
to the dog, who had devoured a generously filled
bowl of stew with such speed that there had been
nothing to do but to give it, rather guiltily, a
second helping. There was plenty in the pot anyway, and she had reason to be glad of this when
Mijnheer Bal returned and Friso, who, between
visits to his patient, had been on foraging
expeditions of his own, joined them. The two
men emptied their plates with almost as much
speed as the dog had done; she gave them more
and went on eating her own smaller helping.
'When did you last have a meal?' she inquired.

Friso looked up. 'Last night. I went to a case
early this morning and didn't stop for breakfast—came straight on here. I should think Bal
is in like case.'

He said something to the other man, who
shook his head and then laughed, and then made,
for him, quite a long speech. Friso translated.

'He didn't have any breakfast either; but he
says he's glad you came, because your cooking
is very good.' He got up and put the plates on
the table, and when she started to get up, said,
'No, stay where you are, I'll get the coffee. You
deserve a rest.' While he was doing it, he said
over his shoulder, 'The police have sent a man

in to Leeuwarden; the telephone is still out of
order.' He glanced at his watch. 'The tide will
be on the turn soon, they should be able to reach
us within the next hour or so.'

He poured the coffee and gave her a mug. He
said on a laugh, 'I never dared to hope that you
were a good cook too.'

She met his twinkling eyes with a composed
air and a racing heart, hoping that her hot cheeks
would be attributed to her efforts over the little
stove. They weren't.

'You're lovely when you blush,' he added.

She drank her coffee in a dream, then, after
taking a look at Mevrouw Bal and the baby,
went to heat water for the washing up. It took
some time and she filled it in by gazing out of
the window at the weather, which hadn't
improved at all. The two men sat silent, puffing
at their pipes with an air of not wishing to be
disturbed—in any case, she could think of
nothing worth while to talk about. She wandered
over to the stairs and looked down and
exclaimed 'Oh!' in a rather thin voice before she
could stop herself. The water had risen—not just
a few inches; the stairs were two-thirds covered.
The water was dark and still and menacing. She
drew back with a shudder and felt the reassuring
touch of Friso's hands on her shoulders.

He said placidly, 'It won't come any higher;
the tide's on the ebb. They'll be able to start

repairing the breach, and this will all be pumped dry in no time at all. This weather can't last much longer.'

She twisted round to look up at him. He looked weary and he badly needed a shave, but the calm of his face wasn't superficial; it went deep inside him. She had been frightened, but now she felt safe. She said so and he raised his eyebrows quizzically. 'That's an illusion,' he said comfortably, 'because of my size. If I had been a small man, you might not have felt so safe.'

Harriet drew a deep breath. 'You're wrong,' she said steadily. 'I should feel safe with you whatever your size.' And in the same breath, 'The kettle's boiling.'

The police arrived first. Two large quiet men, who reflected Friso's calm. They came quietly up the small staircase in their heavy rubber boots and their waterproof coats, saluted the doctor as an old acquaintance, and listened wordlessly to what he had to say. Harriet had been sitting on a pile of blankets with the dog, smelly but warm, beside her. She listened to Friso's quiet voice too—it sounded assured and completely confident; just to hear it was happiness. She caught his eye and smiled, her mouth curved delightfully, her blue eyes shone; she had forgotten the past and the future; the present was enough, here with him.

He stopped what he was saying and looked back at her, not smiling, his face impassive. In a moment he finished talking to the men and spoke to her in English.

'Harriet, I should like you to meet two good friends of mine—Mijnheer Kok and Mijnheer Wijma.'

She scrambled to her feet, and the dog too, and shook the enormous hands held out to her. The dog grinned toothily and blinked at the men with bright eyes. '*De hond*?' queried Constable Kok. She couldn't understand what Friso was saying, but he could see from the expression on the policeman's face that he accepted the explanation. The men laughed and Bal, who was at the window, stopped his laughter to point and say something to Friso. 'The ambulance,' he said over one shoulder, and Friso nodded to her, said, 'See to Mevrouw Bal, will you?' and smiled.

They had already taken down the drip, and Harriet had readied her and the baby for the journey as far as possible; but she went at once to make sure that there was nothing more that needed to be done, and in a minute or two, Friso asked, 'May we come in?'

She held the baby while they lifted his mother on to the stretcher and strapped her firmly on to it. When they were ready, Friso said, 'Let me have him.' She saw that he was wearing a wind-cheater, and strove to speak in a matter-of-fact voice. 'You're going with the patient.' It was a statement of something she had really expected.

He tucked the baby into the crook of his arm and stood while Harriet covered the small creature carefully with the plastic tablecloth she had luckily found earlier in the evening, leaving the solemn sleeping face uncovered.

Friso said quietly, 'Stay here until I come. I'm going to see them safely into the ambulance. Bal will go with them, and the ambulance men, of course. Kok or Wijma will bring me back.'

She nodded, but couldn't forbear from saying, 'The water looks very deep.'

'Well, we don't have to walk, you know. They've got a couple of boats.'

She hadn't thought of that, and smiled her relief. 'I'll be tidying up,' was all she said, and watched them make their cautious way downstairs. It was quiet when they had gone, but she had the dog.

She had everything to rights by the time she heard him returning. The dog's deep growl ceased as he heard Friso's voice, and when he climbed the stairs, it wagged its tail, watching him with hopeful yellow eyes. Harriet said nothing, but in answer to her inquiring look the doctor said cheerfully,

'They'll be in Leeuwarden and tucked up in bed before we're home ourselves. Let's be off.'

She stood silently while he passed the bags

and the Minnett's box to the waiting men below, then obediently started down the stairs, the dog breathing hotly at her heels. The water had ebbed, but not much; she had no idea how deep it was and she had no opportunity of finding out, for Friso was suddenly there and she had been picked up and carried to the boat. The wetness of his jacket damped her cheek, but she could feel the steady beat of his heart beneath it and nothing else mattered; she could have stayed in his arms for ever. Apparently the doctor had no such thought. He dumped her unceremoniously in the boat and then turned to help the dog, who was paddling gamely alongside. It stood between them, and shook itself, making them all a great deal wetter than they were already, then sneezed loudly before curling itself up at Harriet's feet, smelling dreadfully of wet fur.

The wind was dying down at last, although the rain was coming and going in mean little squalls. They climbed the slippery path back on to the road, and the three men fetched the bags and then pulled the boat up on to the dyke. The policemen yawned hugely, grinned and said, 'Till tomorrow,' and went along to their car. The dog, without being asked, had got in with the paraphernalia in the back of Friso's Land-Rover. Harriet sank into the front seat—it wasn't all that comfortable, but after the attic, it was bliss.

Friso didn't talk—for one thing the road was in a shocking condition and needed all his attention, and for another Harriet guessed that he was very tired. The police car stopped in St Annaparochie and the policemen waved gaily as they went past, for all the world, she thought, as though they were all going home from some party. They were almost at Friso's house when he spoke.

'What do you intend to do with this animal?' he inquired. She detected amusement in his voice and it provoked her to answer more sharply than she intended.

'Look after him, of course. His owners—if he ever had any—don't seem to want him. I shall find him a good home.'

'Most commendable,' observed the doctor smoothly, 'but I doubt if Mevrouw Van Minnen will—er—welcome him as a member of the household, even for a short stay. He's a farm dog, you know, with a reputation for fierceness and a lamentable habit of biting people he doesn't like.'

Harriet didn't answer at once. Then, 'You—you don't think anyone would like him for a pet?'

'Decidedly not.' He was very positive.

She sat silent. 'You wouldn't like to have him, would you?' she said at last. 'He'd be nice company for J B and Flotsam.'

She knew it was a forlorn hope, for hadn't he just said that no one would want the poor beast?

Friso slowed down to enter his gateway. 'You know,' he said gently, 'I think perhaps that's a good idea.' His voice gave her no inkling of the probable dog-fights which lay ahead of him. He pulled up in front of the door, there was a light on in the hall, she could see his face in its gentle glow.

'Oh, Friso, thank you. I'll come and see him.'

She saw him grin. 'Rather a long journey from England, I fancy. You'll have to rely on my good nature and regular bulletins from Sieske.'

She looked away. Once she had gone, he would add her to his list of other, perhaps forgotten girls. The thought hurt, but there was nothing to do about it. She said, determinedly cheerful, 'I know he'll be happy with you. I'm very grateful. Thank you for being so kind.' She was unable to keep the relief from her voice. 'I'm sure you won't regret it.'

If she had hoped for wholehearted agreement on his part, she was doomed to disappointment, for he said nothing, but got out of the car and came round and helped her out without breaking his silence, unless she chose to count the low whistle he gave to the dog, who answered it by clambering over the back of the Land-Rover and coming to stand by them, shivering.

The door opened before Friso could reach for

his key. Anna was in the hall, looking large and motherly in a voluminous dressing-gown. She started to talk at once, and although Harriet couldn't understand a word of it, she was lulled by the sympathy in her voice. She had been helped half out of her jacket when she stopped suddenly.

'But I must go back to the Van Minnens.'

'At one o'clock in the morning? I asked the police to call up one of their men in Franeker with their walkie-talkie—he'll take them a message; he will have delivered it by now and everyone will have gone to bed, knowing that you are safe.'

Wim had appeared silently, and the doctor handed him the soaking coats and said, 'Sit down,' to Harriet and started to pull off her boots. 'Ah, yes,' he went on, 'the dog.' He explained at some length, speaking Fries, because Wim and Anna preferred it. They made sympathetic sounds when he had finished, and Wim went away and returned presently with a large towel with which he started to dry the dog.

'Shall I do that?' asked Harriet. 'After all, it's because of me that he's here.'

'Wim likes dogs,' Friso answered shortly, 'so does Anna. You can be sure that he will be dried and fed and bedded down in greater comfort than he has ever known in his life before. You are going to have a bowl of Anna's famous onion soup and then you're going to bed.'

He pulled her to her feet, and smiled down at her, and for a moment Harriet forgot that she would be going away in a few days and would never see him again, and that the future was lonely and hopeless. She smiled back at him, her heart in her eyes.

She sat in the small sitting-room where they had had tea, and drank her soup. Friso had some too, and Anna went silently to and fro, watching eagle-eyed that she ate it all up. Afterwards she sat in a gentle stupor. 'That soup was wonderful,' she murmured. 'I feel as though I've had a glass of brandy,' and sat bolt upright in her chair when Friso said,

'You have. Anna's onion soup is something rather special. She puts in cheese and fried bread and pours brandy over them, then adds the soup. Anna is worth her not inconsiderable weight in gold.'

He got up and took her bowl away and gave her a cup of creamy coffee. She drank it, wondering what he had thought of the stew he had eaten in the cottage. She very much doubted if Anna used anything in tins—it must have tasted terrible to someone who liked his soup made with brandy. . . As though she had said it all out loud, he went on, 'But I never tasted anything better than that stew this evening.'

It was silly to feel so elated. She allowed

herself to be led upstairs by Anna, wrapped in a dream induced by brandy and sleepiness, and the mixture of excitement and fright which she had had to hold in check all the evening. Under Anna's motherly eye, she bathed, donned the proffered nightgown and got into bed, to fall asleep within seconds.

CHAPTER EIGHT

SHE awoke to a pale watery sunshine and sat up in bed and took stock of her surroundings. It was a pretty room—the sort of room the daughter of the house might have had, she supposed. The furniture was eighteenth-century and allied with a pink and white Toile de Jouy. Presently she got out of bed and went to look out of the window. The room was at the back of the house, overlooking the little fountain in the formal garden; even under the half-hearted sky it was a charming sight. She went back to bed, stopping on the way to look at herself in the triple mirror on the dressing-table. She frowned as she studied the nightgown—it was silk, real silk, and trimmed with a great deal of lace. It was just a little too big for her, although a perfect fit for the stunning blonde who had come to Sieske's party—it would probably fit the brunette too, thought Harriet viciously. She got back into bed, a prey to a variety of thoughts, none of them pleasant, and all of them becoming rapidly more and more exaggerated. It was a good thing when a strapping girl with beautiful eyes and lint-coloured hair brought in her morning tea. There was a note on the tray in Friso's handwriting. She read the untidy scrawl. 'Breakfast in half an hour' was all it said.

He was in the hall with the three dogs when she went down. J. B. and Flotsam were standing belligerently on either side of him, eyeing the newcomer with ill-concealed dislike.

'Hullo, Harry,' said Friso. 'Have you a name for your friend? If so will you call him over to you?'

She didn't need to call, for the dog had heard her step on the stair and turned to prance on clumsy paws to greet her. She saw that he had been bathed and combed, and carried all the signs of a dog recently well fed. He sat down beside her, facing the other dogs. She put a hand on his head and he grinned. He belonged.

'I thought Moses would be a good name— the water, you see.'

Friso smiled. 'A splendid name. J. B. and Flotsam will think he's yours; they're more likely to accept him in that case. Shall we go and have breakfast? I've a surgery in half an hour. I'll take you back afterwards.'

He opened a door she hadn't been through before—the room beyond was small, its one big window overlooking the front drive. It was furnished in the style of Biedermeyer—the walnut chairs glowed with polish, as did the heavy side table. There was a peach-coloured cloth and nap-

kins on the breakfast table, palely echoing the
heavy curtains drawn back from the window.
Breakfast, Harriet noted, as she took the chair
Friso held for her, was served in some splendour
and calculated to tempt the most finicky appetite.
Which hers was not. She poured the coffee and
handed Friso a cup and went scarlet when he
said, 'You slept well? You must have found my
sister's nightgown rather on the large side—
she's a big girl, and you, if I may say so, are not.'

Before she could stop herself she blurted out,
'It was your sister's? I thought. . .' and then,
appalled, added, 'I—I beg your pardon.'

His grey eyes held hers across the table. He
said evenly,

'Now I wonder what other idea you could
possibly have had in that pretty little head
of yours?'

She was saved from replying to this unanswerable question by a slight fracas between the dogs.
J. B. and Flotsam had edged towards Moses, and
were now each side of him, showing their teeth,
and he, who could have made mincemeat of
them both, was obviously restraining himself
from doing just that. He was, after all, something
of a guest and despite his tramp's appearance,
retained half-forgotten canine manners. He
showed his own teeth in warning, then dropped
his lip meekly in company with the other dogs,
while Friso called them to account, which he

did in a tone of voice which brooked no dis-
obedience. Peace restored, he apparently forgot
that he had had no reply to his question, for he
began at once to tell her about the accident on
the dyke—a foreign plane, off course, had
crashed and exploded. What with the damage
and the high tide and the gale, it had triggered
off the chain of events which had led them to
spend so long at the cottage under the dyke.
They finished their meal, with Friso talking with
a casual ease which lulled her into believing that
she had imagined the anger in his eyes. He
looked at his watch at length and said, 'I must
go—' then got up and pulled the embroidered
bell rope by the carved open fireplace. 'Anna
shall take you to the sitting-room—if you could
amuse yourself there for an hour or so.' His
glance fell upon Moses. 'Perhaps you had better
take him with you.'

She curled up in a large armchair in the sitting-
room, the dog beside her, and leafed her way
through a variety of glossy magazines, but for
once their contents couldn't hold her attention.
She got up and wandered around, looking at
the books, which seemed to be in a variety of
languages, and studying the portraits on the
walls. An hour seemed a very long time, there
was still five minutes of it left by the carriage
clock on the mantelshelf when she opened the
door leading to the salon and went in. There

was plenty to see here—a glass-topped table on slender legs, displaying a collection of small silver, a great glass-fronted William and Mary china cabinet, its shelves filled with plates and cups and bowls and little figures. She examined everything slowly, picturing Friso living here, surrounded by it all, his ancestors staring down at him from their heavy gilded frames. She turned her attention to these now, and was standing before a full-length portrait of a haughty-looking young woman in a yellow crinoline when the door opened and the doctor came in.

'You didn't mind me coming in here?' Harriet wanted to know.

He closed the door gently behind him and leaned against it. 'No,' he said, 'my house is yours, my dear Harriet.'

She turned back to the portrait, feeling her cheeks warm. He had called her that once before—his dear Harriet—his very dear Harriet. Perhaps it was just a way of talking. . . She looked rather beseechingly at the owner of the crinoline.

'My great-grandmother,' said Friso from behind her. 'A haughty piece—like you.'

She turned without thinking, and found herself within a couple of inches of his excellently tailored waistcoat. She tilted her head the better to make her point. 'I am not haughty,' she said indignantly.

'Let us put it to the test,' he said suavely. It was no use to try and free herself, for he had her fast by the shoulders. She saw him smile before his mouth came down on hers.

'And now tell me exactly what you meant at breakfast.'

She had been floating between heaven and earth—now her dream was doused with the cold water of reality, and because she was an honest girl, she didn't pretend not to understand him.

'It was unpardonable of me, and it was not my business.'

His hands tightened on her shoulders, but he was looking over her head with a curious intentness at his great-grandmother's chilly stare.

'You are sure that it's not your business, Harriet?'

She gulped back all the things she wanted to say. She would regret them bitterly later, and worse still, Friso would regret them too. Far better for them to remain the good friends they had become despite their frequent tiffs; there were only four days left now. She said with a casual friendliness which cost an effort, 'Of course I'm sure. Your friends—girl-friends—aren't my concern, but I hope you find one soon who will make you forget all the others.'

He had strolled over to the window, and stood

with his hands in his pockets, his back to her. 'But I have.' He sounded flippant, and she was quick to hear it. She achieved a laugh. 'Until the next one comes along—I'll get my things, shall I, if you're ready to go?'

She didn't wait for a reply but went quickly upstairs to the charming room she had so happily slept in. As she passed the mirror she gave herself an angry look. 'What a fool you are,' she told her image, and blew her delightful nose with a violence calculated to check the tears she longed to shed.

They went in the Bentley. Friso was going on to Groningen after he had been to see Mevrouw Bal and the baby and he hadn't much time.

'This old girl gets me there and back with time to spare,' he explained.

Harriet observed, 'How nice,' in a hollow voice. It seemed like sacrilege to refer to a Bentley 'T', by Mulliner Park Ward with a registration number barely a year old, as an old lady.

He gave her a quick searching glance. 'Don't worry about Moses,' he said, and his voice was so kind that the tears ached in her throat. 'You'll see him again, you know.' He slowed down to thread his way through Franeker. 'He and Wim are good friends already and he'll be company for us all around the house.'

He drew up outside Dr Van Minnen's house, and dropped a hand over her clasped ones on her knee. 'Thank you for your help last night, Harry. We would have been in a pretty pickle if you hadn't turned up.'

Harriet turned and looked at him; her eyes looked enormous and very blue. 'I'm glad I was able to help, though I am sure you would have contrived something even if no one had come.' There wasn't time to say more, for the front door had been flung open and Mevrouw Van Minnen and Sieske were standing there waiting to welcome them. They all went inside, everyone talking at once and contriving to translate for Harriet as they went. Friso had just finished a rather brisk account of the night's happenings, when Dr Van Minnen came in from his surgery and demanded to have the whole tale again. More coffee was poured, and Friso began his tale once more, but this time in Fries, sitting comfortably back in one of the great armchairs, smoking his pipe, as though he had all day in which to do nothing. Harriet, watching him covertly, thought what a tranquil man he was; he never appeared to hurry, but she supposed that nothing would stop him doing something he had made up his mind to do.

Before she could look away he turned his head and stared across at her and suddenly smiled as though he had made a pleasant discovery. She caught her breath and heard Sieske say, 'Harry, wake up. Those two will talk shop for hours.

I'm sure Friso left a great deal out—start again
and tell us everything from the beginning.'

It took some time, for Sieske had to translate
as she went along, and Mevrouw Van Minnen
asked a great number of questions. She had only
just finished when Friso got to his feet and said,
'Well, I must be off.'

He lifted a hand in general farewell and when
he got to the door called to Sieske to go to the
car with him; there was a medical journal he
wanted his partner to have. They went out of
the door together, and Harriet, who was sitting
by the window, could see them standing on the
pavement deep in conversation. She turned her
back; he hadn't even bothered to smile at her
when he went. She didn't look up when Sieske
returned either, but went on trying to decipher
the morning paper's headlines.

'Friso's taking us down to Amsterdam
tomorrow.' said her friend, 'and he thinks he'll
probably come and fetch us home again too.'

Harriet was up early the next morning and
spent a great deal of time on her face and hair.
She would be wearing the green outfit again,
not, she told herself, because she would be seeing Friso, but because she was going to
Amsterdam and wanted to look as nice as possible. She went down to breakfast, smelling
deliciously of Fête. Everyone else was already
at table, and as she slipped into her seat there

were appreciative sniffs. Dr Van Minnen, deep in his morning paper, glanced over the top of it.

'You're both dressed to kill, I see,' he observed mildly. 'And very nice too.' He smiled at his daughter and Harriet. 'I wish you both a good trip—enjoy yourselves.'

He looked at his watch, drank his coffee and folded his paper neatly. On his way to the door he stooped to kiss his daughter's cheek, waved to Harriet, and disappeared surgerywards. Maggina and Taeike got up too, grumbling that they should have to go to school while everyone else had fun. Taeike said slowly, 'Do you think Friso would take us to Leeuwarden first, before you go?'

Sieske gave a little snort. 'Whatever next! Why should he? It's hard enough for him to find the time to take us as it is.'

'Then why does he?' asked Taeike rebelliously. 'You could quite well go by yourselves.' She went out, banging the door behind her, and Sieske said in answer to Harriet's questioning eyebrows, 'It's all right, she dotes on Friso—you see, she's known him most of her life and hates to be left out of anything he does.'

Harriet would have liked to pursue the subject, but there wasn't time. She went upstairs and put on the fetching turban picked up her handbag and overnight case and ran downstairs again in time to see Friso come in the front door. Her

heart jumped and raced so that her breathlessness
wasn't entirely due to the stairs. He stood in the
hall, impeccably dressed and very assured, and
his 'Good morning, Harriet' was coolly friendly,
only as she got nearer she could see how his eyes
twinkled. 'How very glamorous,' he observed.
'Enough to steal my heart, if you hadn't already
done that.'

She blushed and looked uncertain, almost, but
not quite, sure that he was teasing. It was fortunate for her peace of mind that Sieske and her
mother came out of the dining-room and he
turned, just in time to receive Sieske's nicely
proportioned but not inconsiderable weight in
his arms.

'Friso! You are a dear to take us—I telephoned Tante Tonia and she says you must stay
to lunch. You will, won't you? I said you would.'
She gave him a slow sweet smile. 'We shall be
there long before midday, and you'll have time
enough.'

He gave her an avuncular hug. 'I see that you
have got it all arranged, you scheming girl! Poor
Wierd,' he added in mock horror. 'Has no one
warned him of your true nature?' He gave her a
gentle push. 'Go and fetch your things. Harriet's
sitting here like Patience on a monument.'

Harriet drew her brows together. 'That's quite
inapt,' she said tartly, 'for I'm not smiling at
grief, nor am I turning green and yellow.'

He gave her a mocking smile. 'My apologies to you and Shakespeare, my dear girl. You're neither green nor yellow, and I'm quite prepared to take your word for it that you're not smiling at grief—if you say so.'

Harriet inclined her head slightly, looking, she hoped, remote, but it was lost on Friso, who went to the stairs to bellow at Sieske to hurry herself up and then started talking to Mevrouw Van Minnen in Fries, with a casual apology over one shoulder for doing so. Harriet had the darkling thought that Friso might not be best pleased at taking them to Amsterdam—she would have dearly loved to find out who had suggested it in the first place, but Sieske came racing down the stairs and into the car, and there was no chance to say a word to her. She wasn't sure how she came to be sitting beside Friso; but there was Sieske, sitting in the back of the car, reading a letter from Wierd which she hadn't had time to open, and here he was inquiring if she was comfortable. She said, 'Yes, thank you,' in a meek voice, and he let in the clutch.

He took the route over the great dyke across the Ijsselmeer, and kept up a gentle flow of conversation that needed little answering. Harriet listened to his slow deep voice with its faintly accented English, and tried to imagine what life would be like when she went back to England, and there would be no Friso. It did not bear thinking about, but of one thing she was sure, she would dream no more. She sighed, and stifled the sigh as he said, 'You wretched girl, you're not listening to a word I'm saying; I could have saved my breath.'

'I did hear, indeed I did, but a thought came into my head.'

He was looking straight ahead. 'A very sad thought, I take it.'

'Well, yes. I'm sorry, I'm not very good company.' She peeped at his profile. It looked stern; then he turned and smiled before she could look away and she found herself smiling too.

He said, 'You are at all times a good companion, Harriet, and the only one I want.'

She stared at him, the colour washing over her pretty face. He was looking ahead again. She longed for him to turn his head so that she could see his eyes, although common sense told her that he was unlikely to do so while driving the car past a huge trans-Europe transport at sixty miles an hour. When next he spoke it was over his shoulder to Sieske. 'We'll stop at Hoorn, shall we? We can have coffee at that place over the Weigh House—unless you can think of anywhere you'd rather go.'

Sieske deliberated with her usual placid charm and said, 'Yes, that would be delightful, and if there's a telephone there I'll ring up Wierd— he's going to try and come over to Amsterdam the day after tomorrow.' She subsided into a happy silence, clutching Wierd's letter.

The café over the Weigh House was delightful; it had somehow caught the atmosphere of the little town. Harriet peered out of the window and was quite prepared to agree with Friso when he said that Hoorn hadn't changed very much in the last three hundred years. Presently Sieske went away to telephone.

'How's Moses?' asked Harriet, very conscious of Friso's calm stare across the little table.

'Eating me out of house and home. Oh, don't worry, he'll be worth his keep—I'm sorry for anyone who tries to get into the house uninvited. The three of them would confound the enemy, tear him limb from limb and bring me the pieces in triumph. I think he misses you.'

The softness of Harriet's heart was reflected in her face.

'I shall miss him too,' she said regretfully. She was about to say something else when she caught the doctor's eye. Something in his face set her pulse hurrying. His voice sounded different too.

'And if I tell you that I shall miss you a great deal more than Moses, what will be your answer, my dear Harriet?'

She didn't say anything, because she was unable to think of the right words, but she felt her happiness bubble up inside her and smiled;

not just with her mouth, but with her eyes too.
A small sensible voice inside her head was
reminding her that she was in grave danger of
joining the luscious blonde and the beautiful brunette, and possibly a number of other young
ladies on his list. She turned a deaf ear, for none
of them seemed real; only she and Friso were
real, staring at each other across the table's
width. He smiled. 'You may have cautioned your
tongue to remain silent, but you're quite power-
less to stop your eyes saying what they want to.'
He stretched a hand out to take hers and hold it
fast; it was firm and cool and his touch sent a
tingling up her arm. Sieske came back and he
made no effort to release her, and the pink in
her cheeks deepened, but her friend, after one
swift glance, started a rather involved explanation of Wierd's plans to meet them.

'He's arranged everything,' she said happily.
'You'll be worn out with sightseeing, Harry, but
it's your only chance.'

Harriet avoided Friso's eye. 'You're a dear to
arrange it all, Sieske, and I know I shall love it.
Never mind if it's a rush, I'll have plenty of
time to sort it all out when I get home.'

'You won't, you know,' said Sieske. 'You'll
be far too busy being a ward sister; your head
will be full of cutdowns and operation cases
and getting the off-duty worked out to please
everyone.'

Harriet sighed. 'I'd forgotten. But I'll have off duty and days off.' Sitting there, with Friso's hand over hers, the future looked singularly uninviting; after all, Friso hadn't really said anything to alter it. She cast around desperately for another topic of conversation.

'That reminds me,' she said, and the relief of having thought of something showed on her face, 'I wanted to ask you something.' Her glance in Friso's direction was so fleeting that she quite failed to see the look of amusement on his face. 'You and Mijnheer Bal were talking in that attic and you recited something and he joined in, and you said that if I reminded you, you would explain it to me.'

She tried, with no success at all, to withdraw her hand and felt his fingers tighten. 'Ah, yes. Our ancient Friesian oath; you know it, of course, Sieske.' He started to speak in his own tongue, rolling out the incomprehensible words in his quiet slow voice. When he had finished Harriet said, 'There were two English words— ebb and flood.'

'That's right—our language has a certain similarity to your own. I'll translate it, though it won't sound so splendid. I imagine the men who first uttered it were tough, but they lived in tough times. It goes something like this. "With five weapons shall we keep our land, with sword and with shield, with spade and with fork and with the spear, out with the ebb, up with the flood, to fight day and night against the North-king and against the wild Viking, that all Friesians may be free, the born and the unborn, so long as the wind from the clouds shall blow and the world shall stand".'

Harriet said quietly, 'I like it.' She repeated, '"So long as the wind from the clouds shall blow"—that's for ever.'

'We are a persistent race; we do not give up easily, nor do we let go.' The grey eyes bored into hers. 'For ever is a long time—loving is for ever, too. So long as the wind from the clouds shall blow. Remember that, my dear Harriet.'

She stared back at him. How could she forget, and what exactly did he mean? And now she would probably never know, for he had released her hand and was paying the bill, and telling Sieske that if they wanted to powder their noses they had better hurry up.

For the rest of the journey the talk was of places and things and the world in general. She took but a token share in the conversation while she tried to remember everything that Friso had said, and in consequence became so bewildered that she had to be told twice that they had reached the outskirts of Amsterdam. Tante Tonia had a flat on the Weesperzijde. The houses were tall and narrow with basements and steps up to their front doors; on the other side of the street was the Amstel river, its broad surface constantly ruffled by the laden barges chugging one way or the other—a fact which, to Harriet's way of thinking, more than compensated for the basements. The street was quiet too, trams ran along the main street at the end, it was true, but their noise was quite drowned by the constant, hooting on the river and the peculiar thumping noise of the diesel engines on the barges.

Friso stopped half-way down and told them to go on ahead while he got their bags. They mounted the steps and Sieske pressed the second bell in the gleaming row of bells, each with its little visiting card, at the side of the door. The door gave a click and opened, and they went up the precipitous staircase to the first floor.

Tante Tonia was waiting for them—she was like her sister, but in a large, cosy fashion. Mevrouw Van Minnen was what was commonly called a fine figure of a woman, Tante Tonia was frankly plump, with grey hair severely drawn back from a face whose eyes were still a bright youthful blue; and held only lines of laughter. She greeted them warmly, speaking a fluent, ungrammatical and dreadfully muddled English which nonetheless lost none of its sincerity. The girls were bustled into the sitting-room where Oom Jan repeated the embraces and made them welcome in an English as pedantically correct as an old-fashioned textbook; but

he broke into Dutch as he caught sight of Friso in
the doorway, leaving his wife, after exchanging
greetings with the doctor, to carry off her guests
to the room they were to share.

Ten minutes later, they were sitting round the
square table in the comfortable old-fashioned
dining-room. Harriet had combed her hair and
done things to her face; she settled herself in
the chair opposite Friso, conscious that she was
looking her best, and that she had used just sufficient Fête to surround herself in a tantalizingly
faint cloud of perfume. She saw Oom Jan's nos-
trils twitch appreciatively and caught Friso's eye
across the table. He was smiling, but she didn't
smile back, for she discerned a mocking twinkle
in his gaze; she gave Oom Jan her full attention
and ate a good lunch and tried to pretend, without success, that Friso wasn't there. It was a
relief when they all went into the sitting-room
for coffee, but the relief was tempered by her
knowledge that he would get up and go at any
moment. He did in fact do just that, much sooner
than she had expected. She watched him say his
goodbyes with a sinking heart and listened to
his plans to fetch them in two days' time stifling
a strong desire to go back with him to Franeker.
The time was so short—she would see him once,
perhaps twice before she left. Her gloomy
thoughts were interrupted by his cool voice.

'Come down to the door with me, will you, Harriet?'

She got up wordlessly and followed him out of the flat down the steep stairs. He opened the door and they stood on the top step in the sunshine and because she could not bear the silence any longer she said,

'Please give my love to Moses.'

'Of course. Why did you scowl so at luncheon?'

Harriet examined the pink nails of one hand, and said untruthfully,

'I did not scowl!' and added, 'You were laughing at me.'

'But you have a most endearing habit of making me laugh at you. Didn't you know that?' He possessed himself of one of her hands. 'Shall you be glad to see me when I come to fetch you?'

She looked at him then. He wasn't laughing at her now; his grey eyes were tender and sparkling, but his face was grave. She said equally gravely, 'Yes, I shall be glad to see you again, Friso.'

He kissed her on the mouth with a gentleness she hadn't expected of him. 'Dear Harriet. You still remember the Friesian oath?'

She was still a little breathless from his kiss. 'Yes.'

'Good. So long as the wind from the clouds shall blow—my dear.'

He was gone. She stood on the steps and waved, then went back upstairs, to present to the people waiting there a face transformed by happiness.

CHAPTER NINE

THE next day was a cataclysm of sound and colour, historical buildings, museums and canals. Harriet, sitting beside Sieske in one of the boats touring the canals of the city, craned her pretty neck to see everything, while her ears tried to take in the information offered in Sieske's soft slow voice, Tante Tonia's quick, much louder one, and Oom Jan's precise English, spoken with such deliberation that he was inevitably describing some subject already dealt with by his wife and niece. Harriet nodded agreeably to each piece of information and concentrated on Oom Jan who appeared to know his Amsterdam like the back of his hand. Back on dry land, a brisk altercation, conducted in the friendliest of terms, took place. The ladies, naturally enough, considered that the shops were a vital part of the sightseeing programme, whereas Oom Jan, who detested shopping with females, urged a visit to the Rijksmuseum, followed by a look at the Mint Tower and the Begijnhof Almshouses. He was, of course, doomed to failure. Sieske pointed out in her calm way that the Mint Tower was at the end of the

Kalverstraat, where all the best shops were, and that it would be the easiest thing in the world to turn aside half-way down this fascinating thoroughfare and spend a little time in the Begijnhof, which was a mere stone's throw from it. It was a happy solution, for the ladies left their escort to browse in a bookshop, and spent an agreeable half hour window-shopping, before allowing him to lead them to the Begijnhof. Harriet was delighted with the peaceful little place; it seemed incredible that anything so quiet could exist for centuries in the heart of the bustling city. She wanted most desperately Friso to be there too, so that she could tell him how she felt. Her mouth curved into a happy smile at the thought of seeing him again. The fact that she was leaving in two days' time wasn't important any more; all that mattered was what Friso would say to her before she went. . .

Via the Mint Tower, they crossed the Munt Plein and took coffee in the comparative luxury of the Hotel de l'Europe, so that they could watch the unending traffic on the water; and then made their leisurely way down the Leidseweg towards the museum. It was cool inside the big rooms, and they wandered through their vastness, gazing at a seemingly unending vista of paintings. It was almost one o'clock by the time they had finished, and when Oom Jan suggested lunch in the museum restaurant they lost no time

in following him through the big glass doors and
allowing themselves to be led to a table by the
window. The food was good; soup—real soup,
not out of a tin; Wienerschnitzel with tiny peas
and potatoes creamed to incredible smoothness,
and a sweet composed largely of whipped cream.
Harriet devoured it all with a healthy appetite
and obediently drank the glass of wine she was
offered. Presently, relaxed and revitalized, they
started to plan their afternoon.

'The Palace,' said Sieske, 'and probably
you'll see one of those street organs you asked
about.'

Harriet smiled at her friend, thinking what a
dear she was; she was going to miss her when
she got back to hospital. She dragged her
thoughts away from the future; time enough to
do that in two days' time.

'No good,' said Tante Tonia, 'the Palace isn't
open today—we'll have to fit it in tomorrow.
What about diamonds?'

It was a happy thought. The afternoon passed
quickly, for after a visit to Van Moppes'
diamond showrooms, they walked down some
of the narrow streets lining the canals, peering
into the small shop windows of countless antique
dealers. They took their tea in a very small room
behind a pastrycooks', where the cakes were so
various and rich that Harriet was quite unable
to choose for herself and ate her way happily

through a rich confection of chocolate and cream and nuts which Sieske assured her was delicious; she would have eaten a second of these confections if her host had not looked at his watch and declared that if they didn't go home that minute they would be late.

'What for?' they asked, but he laughed and refused to say, merely exchanging a conspiratorial smile with his wife. It wasn't until they were sitting down doing justice to various cold meats and an enormous bowl of salad that he answered their question.

'I have seats for the Stadsschouwburg—The Netherlands Opera Company are performing *Tosca*.' He smiled, well pleased with the girls' delight and they finished the meal in a little rush of excitement, which augured well for the success of the evening. And success it was— the theatre was bright with lights and pleasantly crowded. Their seats were a little to the side of the circle with an excellent view of the stage. They settled themselves comfortably and whiled what time there was before the curtain went up by studying the audience and discussing what they would do when Wierd arrived the following morning. He would have to go back about tea time, but Sieske was determined to make use of him and his car. A short trip, she thought, before lunch at Scheveningen. Harriet agreed happily to everything suggested. Friso was to come after tea; until then she didn't mind in the least what she did. The curtain rose, and she became absorbed in the music, and perhaps because she was so much in love herself, almost burst into tears as the tragic story unfolded itself.

It was fortunate that the interval intervened and Oom Jan whisked them all away to the foyer to drink something dark red and velvety in a glass, which had the immediate effect of making her feel very cheerful indeed, but later caused her to feel more and more sad at the complications the people on the stage were forced to endure. But by the time the opera was finished she had quite recovered her volatile spirits and was delighted to be taken to a café for coffee before going back to the Weesperzijde, to go to bed and sleep almost immediately, while listening to Sieske's soothing voice from the next bed, still plotting and planning for the next day.

The sun was shining when they got up. It was still early by the time they had had breakfast, but they had barely finished their coffee when Wierd arrived. Sieske went downstairs to meet him, and Harriet wondered if she would have the chance to do the same when Friso arrived that evening. The thought made her smile, so that Wierd wanted to know if it was Amsterdam that made her look so happy, She said seriously,

'Amsterdam is lovely, but Friesland is beautiful.' She looked dreamily out of the window, not seeing the street outside, but Friso, busy with his patients, and only turned round when she heard Sieske say,

'Well, you're going back this evening, Harry. But now Wierd wants to take us to the Keukenhof gardens.' She slipped an arm into that of her fiancé. 'And then perhaps Den Haag—and we can eat at Saur's.'

'That'll be nice,' Harriet said. Indeed, she had only a slim idea as to what the Keukenhof was, and didn't much care, but if it was a pleasant way of passing a day, that was all right. She went to get a jacket and her handbag, wondering if 'evening' meant just after tea or quite late. She wanted very much to ask Sieske if Friso had a surgery to take before he came to fetch them, but she felt shy of talking about him, even to Sieske. She mooned about, doing unnecessary things to her face and hair, and was quite surprised when Sieske put her head round the door, and asked, her usual placidity ruffled, 'Harry, what do you do? You have to fetch only your jacket and bag, and it is already ten minutes.'

Harriet was opening and shutting drawers in a guilty fashion. She turned a rather pink face to her friend, and said,

'I'm sorry, I was thinking about—'

She stopped herself in time, and ended tamely,

'Just thinking.' She looked so contrite that Sieske smiled at her.

'It will be beautiful in the Keukenhof, Harry; it is like Friso's garden, but many hundred times larger.' She went over to the mirror and poked at her pretty hair, missing Harriet's sudden vivid blush.

There was another delay occasioned by Tante Tonia, who gave a good many well-meaning instructions as to how they could reach the Keukenhof in the shortest time and the most suitable method with which to explore it when they got there. When they finally reached the car, Wierd said, speaking in his careful English, 'We have the time to go along the little roads, if you would like, Harry.'

Harriet, sitting in the back and watching a very long, very thin barge glide down the Amstel, agreed very readily to this plan. The motorways were wonderful if you need to get from here to there in a hurry, but it seemed today there was no need of that. They drove through the ordered incomprehensible confusion of Amsterdam's traffic into the comparative quiet of Amstelveen, where they turned off on to a road running along the top of a dyke, which had the double attraction of Schipol on one side of it, and a canal on the other. Harriet, anxious to miss nothing, craned her neck to look at everything her companions felt she should see and listened to Wierd while he gave her a potted history of the Haarlemmermeer Polder. He did it very well, only she did wish that he wouldn't use such long and difficult words—it couldn't be because he wanted to air his English, because he wasn't that sort of man at all. Her ears rang with strange Dutch names from long ago, and detailed accounts of windmills and steam pumps and their uses, as well as a great many useful and interesting facts which Sieske slipped in from time to time. It was a relief to reach Aalsmeer where they stopped for coffee, and explained to her why they weren't going to stop there for her to see the flower auction. 'It'll take a long time to see it properly,' Sieske pointed out, 'and then we should have to hurry round the Keukenhof if we're going to The Hague as well. When you come to visit us again—' she blushed faintly, 'Wierd and me—we can come.'

Harriet said, 'Yes, of course,' and smiled, mostly at her own secret thoughts—perhaps Friso would be with her.

They left Aalsmeer by the same road so that Harriet could have a glimpse of the lake, then Wierd turned down what he described as a local road, bisecting the *polder*, until they came to another canal with its accompany road, which in due time led them to Lisse and the Keukenhof.

Harriet hadn't quite known what to expect, certainly not the blaze of colour which met her

eyes. They got out of the car, and Wierd said,
'No plan, I think? Just to amble?'

Harriet was only too delighted to agree, having already ambled in several directions just to
make sure that everything was real. It was
surprisingly quiet and free from people; the
coachloads and bus tours, said Wierd, would
come about lunch time. They wandered up and
down the paths and along the edge of the water,
where the flowers grew as though nature had
put them there and not astute bulb-growers with
an eye to getting big orders. The water was criss-
crossed with little rustic bridges; they were
half-way over one of these when Harriet's eye
was caught by a group of people coming towards
them from the other side. Well in advance of
the others walked a smallish figure, escorted by
a tall man, talking animatedly. They were very
close to Harriet when she realized who it was.
She looked round rather wildly for Sieske, who
had stopped with Wierd to hang over the bridge
to watch the fish. They were standing with their
backs to the balustrade, looking unconcerned, as
were the few people opposite them. All anyone
had done, as far as she could see, was to move
back as far as possible to make a little more
room. She did the same thing herself a bare
moment before Queen Beatrix walked past,
flashing a pleasant smile as she went, followed
by the members of her entourage, struggling

manfully to keep up the pace. When they had
gone, and the small brisk figure was no longer
visible, Harriet joined the others, open-mouthed.

'That was Queen Beatrix,' she said.

'That's right,' Sieske's voice was as calm and
unhurried as ever it was. 'She comes here
because she loves to look at the flowers too, but
she does not care to make an occasion of it—
she prefers that we do not stare or gather to
watch her.'

'Oh? Well, I'm so glad I've seen her. She
looked charming and just as a queen should
look—she smiled at me too. Who was the man
with her?'

Wierd answered. 'That would be the Directeur
of the Keukenhof, and the people with her are
the members of her household.'

'She walked very fast,' commented Harriet.
'The people at the back were almost running.'

'Our Queen,' said Wierd a trifle pompously,
'is a very energetic person—she is also much
loved by her people.'

Harriet saw that he was slightly hurt and very
much in earnest. She said hastily, 'I'm sorry if
I sounded if I was criticizing the Queen. I didn't
mean to. I like and admire her very much and
I'm very happy to have seen her.' She smiled
at her two friends. Meeting the Queen seemed
a sort of good luck symbol for the future. . .

she sighed on a sudden little glow of happiness and asked,

'Those tulips over there by the trees—they're gorgeous. What are they called?'

Sieske followed her gaze. 'Kaufmanniana,' she murmured knowledgeably. 'Gluck, I think. Is it not so, Wierd?'

He nodded. 'Yellow and carmine—Friso has some in his garden; you will have seen them?' He looked inquiringly at Harriet, who to her vexation felt her cheeks grow hot at Friso's name. But she answered coolly enough, 'So he has, by the pool.' Her words conjured up such a clear picture of herself standing on Friso's veranda with Friso beside her that for a moment she forgot where she was.

Sieske gave her a long considered look. 'You will see them again,' she said positively, and Harriet, certain of it too, flashed a smile that caused Wierd to say, 'How very happy you look, Harriet. It is as though you are in. . .' He didn't finish his sentence, for his future bride had given him an unseen but none the less extremely painful kick on the shin with a well-shod size seven. Rendered speechless with pain, he caught her warning eye; but his drastic reminder had been unnecessary, for Harriet had not been paying attention anyway. She had caught sight of a bed of yellow hyacinths she had admired in Friso's garden. She searched her memory. 'City of

Haarlem,' she said dreamily, and smiled again at nothing at all, not noticing the understanding glances her companions exchanged as they started to stroll along beside her.

'If you come this way,' suggested Wierd, 'there are some daffodils—jonquils. If you remember Friso has them naturalized beside that little path between the glasshouses and the house.'

Of course she remembered. Friso had kissed her by the potting shed and they had walked down that same path together. The three of them stopped by the sweet-smelling bed; its fragrance made memory even more vivid. She beamed at Wierd. 'What a lovely day this is being,' she breathed.

It had turned fine, with a well-washed sky and pale sunshine, which despite its lack of warmth held a promise of summer. It was pleasant amongst the flowers and the newly leafed trees. The storm and flood seemed distant and vague, like some half-forgotten news she had read a long time ago. But it was only three days. Time, she discovered, had very little meaning for her, only in relation to the amount of it she had to spend away from Friso. She no longer cared about the blonde, or the brunette, nor for that matter any other girl he most certainly had known at some time or other. She was a victim of her own dream, and she didn't care.

They got to The Hague in time for lunch.
Harriet had felt a sharp disappointment as they
passed through its suburbs, they were so remarkably unforeign, but as they got nearer the heart
of the city, she could find no fault with it, by
the time they had found somewhere to put the
car and walked up Lange Voorhoust, she was
quite enchanted with it.

Saur's was fun too. They went downstairs to
the smart, expensive snack bar, crowded with
young people like themselves eating delicious
bits and pieces. Harriet left the ordering to Wierd
and was surprised when he asked if she was
hungry. She said simply, 'Yes, of course,' then
added hurriedly, in case he was short of money,
'But a sandwich will do.'

He looked horrified. 'I ask only because you
are so small a person and perhaps eat only a
little.'

Sieske giggled. 'Harry eats like a horse,' she
eyed her friend's fragile form. 'No one know
where it all goes to, for she always looks the
same. If you order the same for her as you intend
to order for us two outsizes, she'll eat every
crumb of it.'

When the food came, her sapient remarks
were completely justified. It seemed the restaurant was noted for its seafood. Harriet ate her
way happily through everything put before her.
She had imagined that, like so many lovesick

women, she would have lost her splendid appetite, instead of which she was enjoying it all very
much. It was after two o'clock by the time they
had finished, and when she noticed the time, her
heart gave a little leap at the thought that there
were only a few hours before she would
see Friso.

Naturally enough, after this pleasant interlude,
the girls found it imperative to do a little window
shopping. They admired the hats—unpriced in
Van Dooren's window; speculated as to the cost
of the fur coats in Kulme's, and were only dis-
suaded from going into La Bonneterie to inquire
the price of an enchanting organza dress by
Wierd, who pointed out that unless they intended
to spend the rest of the day looking at clothes,
which, he pointed out reasonably, were obtain-
able anywhere and probably far cheaper than in
s'Gravenhage; it was high time they were on
their way to Scheveningen.

Their combined efforts to make him see the
silliness of his remarks about clothes being the
same anywhere lasted until they reached the car,
and, as far as they could see, had no success
at all.

The sea looked cold; slow, pale blue waves
rolled in steadily on to the wide sands. The three
of them walked along the sea front, the wind
tangling their hair; it had a nip in it which made
them step out briskly. They admired the hotels

lining the broad road, and gazed at the famous
pier, then turned back to walk the other way so
that Harriet could see the fishermen's wives in
their costume. She wished she had brought her
camera; instead, she bought a great number of
postcards; it was amazing what a lot of people
there were to whom she hadn't sent this proof
of being abroad. They went back to the car at
length, discussing where they should have tea.
Sieske's quiet persistence won the day and
Harriet found herself back at The Hague, taking
tea amidst the Victorian splendour of Maison
Krul. It was a leisurely little meal and inevitably
the talk was of the wedding. When they at length
got up to go, Wierd decided to go back to
Amsterdam on the motorway. 'I don't know
what time Friso is coming,' he said, 'but I don't
suppose he'll want to wait around, and I must
get back myself.'

They shared the motorway with a horde of
other drivers, all presumably competing in a Le
Mans of their own. Wierd apparently shared
their ambition, for he did his best to out-Jehu
them; it seemed with some success, for as they
reached the outskirts of Amsterdam, he looked
at his watch and announced with quiet pride that
he had knocked off three minutes of his previous
record. Harriet, who was a tolerable driver herself, applauded his efforts, and acquitted herself
so well in the ensuing conversation that he con-

fided to Sieske afterwards that for a foreigner,
her friend Harriet was a very sensible girl, as
well as being pretty, if you happened to like
small women. Sieske smiled at him fondly and
said nothing. She was very fond of Harry, and
she liked everyone else to like her too; they
almost always did

It was still quite early as they rounded the
last corner into the Weesperzijde. There were
already a great many cars parked along the side
of the street, none of them Friso's Harriet felt
disappointment like a physical pain take pos-
session of her. The faint hope that he had parked
somewhere else and was in the flat waiting for
them was quickly dispelled when they arrived
at the top of the stairs and found Tante Tonia
standing at her door. Quite a few minutes were
wasted while she wanted to know if they had
had a good day and had the weather been fine
and what did they think of the Keukenhof this
year. When, after what seemed like hours to
Harriet, they went into the sitting-room it was
to find it empty. She went a little pale, fending
off a premonition that something, somewhere,
had gone wrong. Her dismal thoughts were cut
short by Tante Tonia asking her if she was tired.
'For you look rather white. It is perhaps good
that you do not return to Franeker this evening.'
She smiled at them both, a bearer of what she
thought was good news. 'Friso telephoned—he

regrets that he cannot come for you. I am to tell you you will be fetched tomorrow morning, after breakfast.'

Harriet felt a little better. It was a bitter disappointment, but tomorrow morning wasn't far off. He must have been called out on a case or got held up in some way. Being a doctor's daughter, she was able to think of half a dozen causes which could upset the best laid plans. She cheered herself up with this reflection, and resolutely ignored a niggling doubt at the back of her mind that there was something. . .

It was half-way through the evening meal that she found herself wondering if he would telephone, and apparently Sieske had thought the same thing, for when Oom Jan suggested a walk and a cup of coffee, she asked if there was anyone to take a message if they were out.

'But why should he telephone again?' asked Oom Jan reasonably. 'He has already said what he had to say, and tomorrow morning you will go home.'

There was no argument against his logic. They fetched their coats, and accompanied their host and hostess down the stairs and out on to the pavement, where they turned their faces towards the imposing pile of the Amstel Hotel. It was a pleasant evening, cool and windy, and the Amstel, still loaded with traffic, reflected the evening sky and gave a glow to its surroundings.

They turned the corner and went over the bridge and past the hotel. Harriet had a good look at it as they went slowly past. It looked remote and welcoming at the same time; she thought that she would like to stay there and wondered if she ever would. They crossed the Amstel again and turned their steps towards the centre of the city, and Tante Tonia and Oom Jan argued equably as to which was the best place to have coffee. They settled for the Haven restaurant, which was thirteen floors up and afforded a fine view of the whole city, so that Harriet almost forgot how unhappy she was and spent a delightful hour picking out landmarks under the others' guidance. They had drinks as well, and a great many sorts of tiny savoury biscuits to nibble. She had advocaat and enjoyed it very much.

Surprisingly, she slept all night, although her last troubled thoughts had been of Friso. He hadn't telephoned while they had been out; there was no need to do so this morning. It was the first thing that she thought of when she awoke— that he would be coming in a few hours' time. She lay in bed, impatient of the clock, and at last got up earlier than usual on the pretext of writing another batch of postcards; it was better than doing nothing. Sieske woke up after half an hour or so, stretched and yawned and lay watching her friend. 'I shall miss you very much, Harry,' she said at length. 'Just because you are going back to England our friendship does not end, you understand?'

Harriet put down her cards—it was a dull job, anyway—and said with emphasis, 'Of course not, Sieske. You'll both be over to see us as soon as you can, won't you?'

'First you will be here, Harry, for you will be bridesmaid at my wedding.'

'So I shall,' said Harriet briskly. 'And that's only a month or two away. I must book my holidays.'

She paused. Hospital, that small world of its own, seemed unimportant. If—no, when she went back, it would absorb her ruthlessly and become her way of life again.

She jumped visibly when Sieske said idly, 'I wonder why Friso didn't come yesterday. It must have been something serious to keep him. He told me that he would come.' She turned a vague gaze upon Harriet. 'Did he not say so to you also?'

Harriet found her tongue. 'Yes, he did. I—I wondered too.'

Sieske got slowly out of bed and wandered around the room in search for her stockings. 'Well,' she remarked cheerfully, 'we'll soon know, for he'll be here after breakfast.'

The remark threw Harriet into a fever of activity. The cards were forgotten; she padded along to the bathroom on urgent feet, decided that her

nails were in need of a manicure, and having
put her hair up with extraordinary care pulled
it all down again, declaring that she looked a
complete fright. Throughout this exhibition of
nerves on her part, Sieske had continued to dress
herself without haste, making appropriate soothing noises at intervals, and contriving to get her
down to the breakfast table not more than five
minutes late. As they were leaving the bedroom
she stopped in the doorway and looked back
over a shoulder. 'He feels exactly the same as
you do, Harry. At least, I'm almost sure he
does—I've known him a long time.' She smiled
into her friend's suddenly pink face and led the
way to the dining-room.

For once, Harriet's splendid appetite had
failed her, she sat at the table watching the
minute hand crawl around the clock's face,
making a roll last a very long time, and talking
so much that no one noticed that she wasn't
eating; but how could she eat when she was so
happy? They had finished at length and the two
girls were standing at the window when a car
drew up in front of the house. It was neither the
AC 428 or the Bentley, but Dr Van Minnen's
BMW.

'It's Father,' exclaimed Sieske, and then,
'And Maggina and Taeike.' She sounded
puzzled, but went at her usual unhurried pace
from the room. Harriet stayed where she was by

the window, fighting a childish desire to burst into tears of disappointment, and what was worse, a growing unease. She tried not to look too eagerly at the doctor as he came into the room, and fancied that he looked uneasily at her, although he sounded as cheerful as usual.

'Good morning, Harry. You see we have all come to fetch you home. The girls are free today, and months ago I promised that I would take them to see the Dam Palace, and here we are. We shall drink coffee first, eh?' He looked at his sister-in-law. 'And then we will spend a little time at the Palace before we go back to Franeker. You will like that?' He added carefully, 'Friso regrets that he could not come.'

She ignored that and said, 'The palace? How lovely.'

Her voice sounded full of false enthusiasm in her own ears, but apparently no one else thought so, for the talk went on uninterrupted around her and lasted right through coffee and their good-byes and during the car ride to the Dam Square.

It was while they were inside the palace that Harriet found herself standing with Taeike at one end of the windows. They were in one of the salons and had turned their backs upon the glories of its Empire furniture and yellow brocade, to gaze at the bustle of the city all around them. Harriet was struggling to carry on a conversation without much success, for Taeike was

proving a difficult companion, and Harriet's
efforts were not perhaps as wholehearted as they
might have been, for her mind was full of Friso.
There was something wrong—very wrong; he
could have telephoned or sent a note by Dr Van
Minnen. He had done neither. They had parted
the best of friends—more than friends, for there
had been a promise of something more than
friendship between them. She gave her head a
weary little shake and asked a completely
unnecessary question about the street organ in
the square below. Her question wasn't answered,
instead, Taeike said, 'Friso takes Vader's surgery this morning.'

The niggling doubt in the back of Harriet's
mind resolved itself into something icily tan-
gible, sending chilly fingers down her spine
to make her shiver. She said merely, 'Oh?' and
waited.

'Yesterday I saw him.' Taeike looked sideways at Harriet, who met the look with a
credible smile.

'Did you? I expect he was busy.'

'No, he was at home, and not busy at all. I
know why he did not wish to come yesterday.'
She hesitated, struggling with her English. 'It is
secret.'

'Then we shouldn't talk about it, should we?'
said Harriet crisply, longing to do just that. 'Just
look at all those pigeons!'

Taeike ignored this obvious red herring. 'It is secret, yes,' persisted the Dutch girl. 'But I think not for you, for you go away tomorrow—and I think also that you do not tell secrets if you say that you will not.' She eyed Harriet shrewdly. 'And you will not tell, not even to Friso, that you know?'

The icy fingers had gone, leaving a hard cold lump in her chest. So there was something. . . the sooner she knew the better. 'Very well,' she said cheerfully. 'Although I think you should have told Friso first; and I can't understand why you should want to tell me.'

It had cost an effort to sound cheerful, but when Taeike reiterated, 'You promise you will not tell—and that you will not say to Friso that you know?' she answered readily, 'I promise that I won't say a word.'

She smiled at the pretty face beside her; after all, it was hard to keep a secret when you were little more than a child. She braced herself against bad news. Perhaps Friso had to go away—or could he be ill? She discarded the thought as ridiculous; Friso was so obviously never ill.

'He is going to be married,' said Taeike.

Harriet was looking at the street organ. She would, she knew, remember every detail of it until the day she died. It was playing 'The Blue Danube'; the strains of music came faintly upwards through the closed windows —a tune she had always liked. It seemed a very long time before she heard her voice say, 'Is he? But why is that a secret? Most—most people marry.'

She steeled herself to look at Taeike as she spoke, and was puzzled at the expression on her face. It could have been pity, mixed with a kind of speculation. Harriet turned her head again and looked out of the window again, without seeing anything at all of what was going on outside.

'You like Friso.' It was a statement, not a question.

Harriet closed her eyes and became aware that the pounding in her ears was the pounding of her heart. She didn't want to believe a word of what Taeike had said, but at least she would have to hear her out. She said evenly, 'Yes, I do. You do too, don't you, Taeike?'

The girl beside her lifted her head proudly. 'I have known Friso since I am little—always we are friends; therefore you understand why he tells me. He says to me, I do not see Harriet again—she is too nice; too—too *deftig*.' Taeike used a word which Harriet recognized as meaning dignified and respectable and decorous. 'You are not, he says, a flirt, but a good friend. He wished to tell you of his marriage, but he knows that you like him. . .' She stopped, and then said softly, 'I'm sorry, Harry.'

Harriet went on looking out of the window at

nothing at all. She knew now how people felt when they died of shame, because it was happening to her too. She clutched her handbag very tightly because she wanted something to hold on to. She had to think clearly, but it had become difficult to think at all. There was a question she had to ask, too.

'Taeike, Friso could have told me this himself.'

The pretty little face was sympathetic. 'Yes, that is so. But perhaps he thinks that as you go away for ever tomorrow, it is nicer—kinder for you like this.' She frowned. 'He has only to say that he is too busy. . .you see?'

It made sense in a horrid sort of way. Harriet swallowed the unpalatable truth. Her dream had shattered around her, and really she only had herself to blame; what had been a couple of weeks' friendship for Friso she herself had glorified into something much more serious—and he had been the one to see it. But why had he said the things he had? She tried to think about it and concluded that it wasn't until after he had said them that he had realized that she wasn't just having fun with a holiday flirtation. She couldn't bear to think about it any more; it was a relief to see the rest of their party advancing towards them, for she realized that further conversation, such as it was, was quite beyond her.

CHAPTER TEN

THE rest of the day was unending. Harriet had
the sensation of listening to her voice and watching her own actions as if they were those of a
stranger, but apparently her behaviour was
entirely normal, for no one made any comment;
she supposed that she was saying and doing the
right things. Fortunately there had been a great
deal to talk about in the car on the way back to
Franeker and she had joined in the chatter with
a feverish animation that she hoped would drown
her other feelings. This hadn't been the case, of
course, but at least it had prevented her thinking
anymore about the conversation in the palace.
They got back for a late lunch, rendered even
later by the number of questions and answers
which Mevrouw Van Minnen asked and
received. Harriet went to her room afterwards
on the pretext of packing, something that she
could easily do in a few minutes, but she wanted
to think. Just half an hour by herself and she
might be able to sort out the situation, for to
accept it without a struggle seemed to her to be
very poor-spirited. She put her case on the bed
and began half-heartedly to empty a drawer, but

she had barely had time to open it before there was a knock on the door and Aede's voice asking if he might come in. She called to him in a falsely cheerful voice and summoned up a welcoming smile as he opened the door.

'Aede, how nice to see you again. Have you got the day off?'

'No. Urgent family business,' he laughed. 'Father told me about your adventure at Bal's cottage. What an experience to have on holiday! Did you mind very much?'

'Mind? Oh, no. I was frightened, but there was so much to do.'

He crossed the room and stood looking down into the street. 'I heard all about Moses too. Friso told me; he thought it most amusing.' He seemed to notice the case for the first time. 'What are you doing?'

Harriet picked up a handful of tights. 'Packing.'

'Now? It'll only take a few minutes surely, and you can do it this evening or even tomorrow morning. I've got the car and I don't have to be back until six o'clock or thereabouts. Let's go for a run and you can bid a temporary good-bye to Friesland. You're coming over for Sieske's wedding, aren't you?'

'Of course.' As she said it, she wondered how she would be able to avoid returning. She would hate to miss her friend's wedding, but she didn't want to see Friso... Yes, she did want to see him; but not with another girl. She smiled at Aede, which encouraged him to say with some awkwardness, 'I'm thinking of getting engaged myself—a girl I met in medical school; so you'll have my wedding to come to too. Not yet, of course—in a year maybe. 'Now, are you coming out?'

Harriet tied a scarf over her hair and picked up a cardigan.

'Yes, I'd love to, and you must tell me all about your girl.'

They went downstairs and found Sieske in the hall, and stood talking for a minute or so, Harriet wasn't paying much attention to what was being said, nor did she see the understanding look the brother and sister exchanged.

Aede didn't ask her where she wanted to go but went straight out of the town towards Leeuwarden, and rather to her surprise, right through it and on to the Groningen road. It was a broad motorway, but the country on either side was delightful, green and placid. Just looking at it had the effect of calming Harriet so that presently she found herself listening with real interest to Aede's plans for the future.

After half an hour he turned off the road and started to make his way back in the direction of Leeuwarden through a series of small country lanes.

There weren't many villages, nor were there many people.

'Milking time,' said Aede, and pointed out the clusters of cows gathered round the milking machines in the fields.

'Where will you live when you marry?' Harriet asked.

'Franeker. Eventually I shall take over from Father, you know. In the meantime there is plenty of work for the three of us. I shall enjoy working with Friso, he's a good chap. We shall be passing his house in a minute or two. Would you like to stop?'

Harriet said, 'No, thank you,' in a quiet voice. If Taeike had been wrong and there had been a misunderstanding, she had no doubt that Friso would discover it and put it right; if not, she would make no move. For the hundredth time she tried to remember if she had said or done anything. She could think of nothing, only that she had let Friso see her feelings.

'Here it is,' said Aede, and there it was indeed. Friso's house, looking lovelier than ever in the spring sunshine. He slowed down as they passed, but she scarcely noticed that as she searched the grounds for a sign of life. There was no one to be seen, but as they rounded the corner and passed the gates, a dog barked.

'That's Moses,' she said. 'I—I thought I should see him before I went home.'

Her companion negotiated a milk float drawn by a plodding horse which had no intention of giving up the crown of the road.

'I don't see why you shouldn't. Did Friso say so? He did? Then you will, Friso is a man of his word, come what may.'

This remark had the effect of making her feel a little more cheerful, they arrived back at the house almost gaily, and the gaiety lasted through her good-bye to Aede and the unexpected influx of the doctor's friends who had come to wish her God-speed, and stayed for drinks. The *burgemeester* and the *dominee* arrived within a few minutes of each other, and in turn, engaged her in conversation. Neither of them mentioned Friso. Behind her smiling attentive face, she struggled to think of some way of introducing him into the talk, but she was given no chance, for the *burgemeester* talked about a production of 'She Stoops to Conquer' which he had seen at Chichester the previous year, and the *dominee* discussed the art of making jam, of all things. Friso had never mentioned Chichester to her and she had strong doubts as to whether his knowledge of jam-making had ever reached more than a theoretical level. Without changing the subject in a most noticeable manner, she could see no way of dragging his name into the conversation. It was left to the beautiful blonde who had arrived without Friso to utter his name. Harriet

had found herself in a corner with the elegant
creature, where they carried on a strictly basic
conversation about clothes—a safe subject for
women in any language. Harriet admired her
companion's white mini-dress; there was little
of it, but what there was was superbly cut.

'Dior?' she hazarded vaguely, anxious to
please the beautiful creature and feeling
strangely incapable of jealousy towards her.
After all, she had arrived with an escort of two
young men whom she had treated with a great
deal more warmth than she had shown Friso.
She couldn't be the girl he intended to marry.
Harriet checked the thought sternly. Thinking
about it could come later.

The blonde smiled. 'You like? Italy. My uncle
buys for me.' She waved vaguely in the general
direction of the room before them. There were
several gentlemen who could have been her
uncle; it didn't seem worth the trouble of finding
out, however. Harriet decided to abandon the
subject anyway; she was searching feverishly for
a topic that could be dealt with easily in simple
English, when her thoughts were brought to a
stunned halt by her companion. 'Friso is silly,'
she pronounced. 'He will not come with us. He
says he is busy. That is not so—' she shrugged
her shoulders. 'He sits alone—with dogs.' Her
tone implied that she had no opinion at all of a
man who sat with dogs in preference to taking

her out. She looked at Harriet with interest. 'You are red; very red. Not well, perhaps?'

'I am warm,' said Harriet faintly. 'The room is warm, are you not warm?' She stopped, aware that she sounded like a Latin grammar. She was having trouble with her breathing too. She said in an urgent voice,

'Friso is ill?'

'Ill? Huh!' The small sound obviously meant the same in both languages. 'Friso is never sick,' the girl laughed gaily. 'You do not know him well, or you would not ask.'

Harriet sighed. 'No,' she agreed in a small voice, 'I don't think I do.' She was glad to be borne away by the curator of the Planetarium to give him her opinion of Friesland and Franeker in particular. It prevented her thoughts from straying.

It was late when she went up to bed. Long after the last guests had gone, they had stayed up talking, and she had watched the clock, willing it to slowness in case Friso should still come. But he didn't, and when at last she was in bed she had to admit to herself that she wasn't going to see him again. Taeike had been right, after all. There was no question of him coming in the morning. Her train left Leeuwarden at half past seven, the doctor would drive her to the station to catch it; no one in their senses would come calling at six o'clock in the morning. She lay thinking about him and her lovely ruined dream, too unhappy to cry.

She fell asleep just before dawn, so heavily that Sieske had to shake her awake. She went down to breakfast, her pretty face without colour and so woebegone that Mevrouw Van Minnen thought that she was in no condition to travel, and suggested that she should postpone her journey.

Harriet begged her not to worry. 'I'm always like this before I go on a journey, aren't I, Sieske?' She added mendaciously, 'I feel marvellous.'

Sieske gave her a long look across the table and said comfortably, 'Yes, Harry dear.' She turned to her mother and explained at length.

Harriet wondered exactly what she was saying, but whatever it was, it convinced Mevrouw Van Minnen, who nodded and smiled, apparently satisfied. Maggina and Taeike had come down too, not to eat their breakfasts, it was too early for that, but to say good-bye. Sieske was going to the station anyway—she would have gone the whole way to the Hoek if Harriet had not firmly declared that she could manage the trip very well by herself.

Harriet finished her breakfast and went upstairs to get the presents she had brought from England and had saved until this moment—Blue Grass cologne for Mevrouw Van Minnen, tobacco for the doctor, undies for Sieske which she had admired when they had gone shopping together in England, and wisps of nighties for Maggina and Taeike. She offered her gifts shyly and begged everyone not to open them until she had gone, but Taeike would not wait. She tore her parcel open with all the impetuosity of youth and stood staring at the pretty trifle, then looked quite wildly at Harriet, who said gently, 'I do hope you like it, dear. You are so pretty.'

'Thank you, Harry. It's beautiful.' She covered it carefully with its tissue paper. 'You think I am pretty?'

'Yes, I do. When you are quite grown up I think that you will be lovely.'

Taeike's eyes filled with tears. She held out her hand, barely touched Harriet's fingers, and dropped it to her side again. 'I must have my bath. Good-bye, Harry.' She didn't look at her at all, but went quickly out of the room, her parcel under one arm. If there had been more time, her strange conduct might have caused comment, but Mevrouw Van Minnen was answering the telephone, and the doctor was already on his way to fetch his car. Maggina said good-bye too and Harriet and Sieske went upstairs to fetch their hats and coats. Harriet was ready first and went downstairs, where she stood by the window in the sitting-room, waiting for the car. She could just see the small alleyway which housed the garage the doctor used. The bonnet of his car was nosing out into the street just as another car flashed past it and drew up with a harsh squeal of brakes at the front door. It was the AC 428, and Friso and Moses got out of it. Harriet whispered, 'Friso, oh, Friso!' but remained rooted to the spot, regrettably aware that she should be formulating some plan or other to meet the situation. Instead she watched him cross the pavement and mount the two steps to the door with Moses at his heel. He did this unhurriedly and she had time to note that he was quite collected in manner, and, despite the early hour, presented an immaculate appearance. She turned her back on the sight of him and faced the door. She could hear his deep voice mingled with the laughing protestations of Mevrouw Van Minnen, accounted for, no doubt, by the presence of Moses. She glanced at the Friese clock on the wall; it was almost time to go. She was picking up her handbag when the door opened and Friso and Moses came in. She longed to run to him, but instead she said brightly,

'Hullo, Moses,' and the beast pricked his ears at her voice and shambled across the room to lean against her, looking up into her face with every sign of pleasure in his own ugly one. She flung her handbag down again and gave him a hug, and said from the safe vantage point of his furry shoulder,

'Hullo, Friso. Thank you for bringing Moses.'

He hadn't moved from the door, but stood watching her, an expression she couldn't read upon his face. But when he spoke his voice was friendly enough.

'I said that you should see him before you went back to England, did I not? I saw no reason to break my word.'

She would have liked to have contested this statement. Had he not said that he would come to Amsterdam to fetch them home? She opened her mouth to say so, then closed it again because the look on his face had become all at once forbidding and arrogant and she had the uneasy feeling that if she attempted to cross verbal swords with him now she would come off much the worse. She said instead,

'Is he good? I hope he'll be happy.' She pulled an ear and Moses licked her hand. She had to admit that a miracle had occurred since he had become a member of Friso's household. His rough coat shone with brushing, he held his stump of a tail with pride, and he had already begun to fill out; even his teeth looked less fearsome. As if aware of her scrutiny, he grinned, blinked his small yellow eyes and licked her again.

She said soberly, 'I shall miss him,' to be chilled by Friso's cool voice, 'That would hardly be possible after such a short acquaintance.' He stared at her. 'In any case, I am sure that Sieske will give you news of him when she writes to you.'

So Taeike had been right after all! She lifted her chin and smiled across at him. It had been delicately put, but she was as capable of taking a hint as the next one. 'I'm sure she will. I shall look forward to hearing about him.'

She saw him look at the clock, and said quickly before he could say it,

'I have to go. I've had a lovely holiday, you have all been so kind.' She paused because she could hear her voice wobbling and that would never do. She hadn't realized until that moment that tyrannical convention was forcing her to say all the right and proper things, while she wished to say only what was in her heart.

Friso put out a hand and she prevented herself just in time from putting her own out when he said,

'Shall I have the lead? Just in case Moses wants to follow you.'

She gave the dog a final hug and put the lead into Friso's outstretched hand, carefully not touching it. Her chest ached with the tears she was determined to hold back. She reached the door and he stood aside and let her go past. With her hand on the handle she forced herself to face him. Even then she would have said something, but his detached, faintly mocking air was dis-

couraging. Alas for her dream! She swallowed,
and said merely,

'Well, good-bye, Friso. I hope. . .' She
stopped, not at all sure what she did hope.

Friso's mouth twisted in a wry smile.

'Well? What do you hope, Harriet? Health,
wealth and happiness, I suppose.' His usually
quiet voice had a nasty edge to it.

They were standing close to each other, the
dog between. She could see the little sparks in
his eyes and knew that he was angry. She said,

'Yes, that is what I truly hope for you, Friso,'
and this time she didn't care how much her voice
wobbled. She wrenched the door open and
whisked through, intent on getting away before
the ache in her chest dissolved into tears. She
heard Moses whine, but Friso didn't wish her
good-bye.

CHAPTER ELEVEN

MEN'S Surgical had been busy all day; theatre cases, admissions from Casualty, a cardiac arrest in the middle of ward dinners. Harriet came back from her seven o'clock supper and started her final round. The nurses were clearing the ward ready for the night; filling water jugs, tidying away the papers and bits of string and old envelopes and orange peel which had accumulated since the afternoon. She went round slowly, looking carefully at each patient and stopping to chat with most of them. Old Mr Gadd, perceptibly weaker, but still demanding cups of tea at unsuitable times, kept her talking for several minutes. It was almost eight o'clock when she finally reached her office and sat down to fill in the Kardex for the night staff. She got up again almost immediately and opened the window, for it was a lovely May evening, and warm. She had been back two weeks from Franeker—it seemed like two years, and very long years at that. She sat down again, not attempting to work. Her desk was very neat and tidy; she looked at it and reminded herself that this was what she had wanted more than anything else—a ward sister's post. Now she had it, and it no longer appealed to her in the least.

It was a pity, she told herself roundly, that she had ever gone to Franeker and become so unsettled. She glowered at her blotting paper and saw Friso's face clearly upon it, and when she shut her eyes to dismiss it, he became even clearer beneath her lids. She sighed, opened them again and began to write. She had always supposed that hearts broke quickly, but it seemed that it was a slow, painful business. The door opened behind her, and without looking round, she said,

'Please pass me Mr Moore's chart, Nurse.' She studied it for a minute. 'Will you take his BP and pulse? They're due at eight.' Mr Moore was the cardiac arrest, recovered now, but needing constant care. The nurse said, 'Yes, Sister.' The door closed behind her and Harriet went on writing, concentrating fiercely. Presently the door opened again, and she asked,

'Well, Nurse?' and turned her head and smiled from a face which had, since her holiday become both pale and thin.

The nurse made her report, wondering, as a great many other nurses were wondering, what Haughty Harry had been up to while she was away. She was just as kind and sweet and hard-working as she had always been, but everyone agreed that she had somehow lost her sparkle.

After the nurse had gone, Harriet sat at her desk, doing nothing, waiting for the night staff to come on duty, her thoughts busy with the day's work. It had been as all the other days, and yet not entirely satisfactory. She tried to put a finger on the cause of her disquiet and couldn't. It was true there had been that terrible moment when Mr Sellers, one of the consultants, had arrived unexpectedly, and come upon her doing nothing, and on the desk before her a sheet of paper with Friso's name written upon it a dozen times, because just to write it had made him seem less hopelessly far away. Mr Sellers had looked at her handiwork without appearing to do so and then asked,

'Settled down, have you, Sister? No regrets? Can't think why a pretty girl like you should want to wear an apron and cap instead of marrying.'

She had gone a slow painful scarlet and made some silly remark about a career, and he had laughed kindly, and said, 'What, no young man in Holland?' Her denial had been far too quick and hot; she realized that now. And Matron— Harriet knitted her brows in puzzlement. She had done her usual ward round, but instead of the formal, gracious leavetaking at the ward door, she had hesitated and made the astonishing request that Harriet should make out the next two weeks' off duty and send it down to the office forthwith. What was more she had been requested to make up the mending book and the instrument and stationery books too, none of which was due for another week. Matron had offered no explanation and Harriet had supposed at the time that it was some new scheme she hadn't known about—she was, after all, new to her job. All the same, if she hadn't known it to be a ridiculous idea, Matron had behaved exactly as though she expected her new ward sister to be on the point of leaving. Harriet wriggled uneasily on her chair, remembering Matron's query as to whether Staff Nurse Wilson was completely reliable. Perhaps Wilson was to be offered a ward—but there was none vacant, Quiet steps on the stairs heralded the night nurses. Harriet, glad to have her thoughts interrupted, opened the Kardex, and turned to greet them.

Half an hour later she was at the hospital entrance, waiting for William. She had two days off—it would be nice to go home and potter around the house and garden, and perhaps help her father in the surgery. Her thoughts, never far from Franeker, went back to the morning when she had been helping Dr Van Minnen and Friso had come in. She closed her eyes the better to remember every small detail, so that her brother, who had just arrived, had to shout from his car to attract her attention. She got in meekly and said, 'Sorry, William, I didn't see you.'

He slammed the door shut for her. 'That's all right, old girl. My fault—I'm late.'

Harriet nodded understandingly, knowing from a lifetime of living in a doctor's household that it was no use expecting punctuality for meals or appointments or birthday treats... broken bones and babies and diabetic comas saw to that. She asked with real interest,

'Anything nasty or just backlog?'

'Backlog,' he said shortly. They had to wait at the traffic lights and he turned to look at her. 'How's things with you? You look whacked.'

She replied suitably to this brotherly observation and lapsed into silence as he weaved a way through the city and out on to the road towards the moors. Indeed, she was silent for most of the journey, but as her brother was fully occupied in describing the charms of a particularly interesting girl he had met while he had been on a course in Bristol; it went unnoticed. Only as he drew up with his usual jolt and gave a telling note on the car horn to signal their arrival to the family did he remark,

'You're peaked. You must be sickening for something.'

Harriet made haste to deny this. 'Of course I'm not, William—I told you, I'm just tired.' There was an edge to her voice; he heard it and frowned. She was his favourite sister and she wasn't at all her usual serene self.

She used the same excuse for her mother, who, however, wasn't so easily satisfied with her explanation.

'Harriet told me she was tired,' she mused as she and her husband were getting ready for bed. 'She's never tired—not that sort of tired,' she added obscurely. 'And you're not going to tell me that she finds her job too much for her.'

Her husband yawned. 'I had no intention of telling you anything, my dear, but our Harry has certainly lost her zest for life. Anaemic, perhaps?'

Harriet's mother gave him a withering look. 'Anaemic!' she snorted. 'She's in love, of course. She looked like this when she came home from her holiday and everyone said it was the journey. It's that partner in Franeker—that Dr Eijsinck. She mentioned him in every letter, but she's not so much as breathed his name since she came back.'

'Couldn't you ask her?' queried the doctor.

His wife paused in her hair-brushing. 'No, dear. She'll tell me if and when she wants to.' She started brushing again with unnecessary vigour. 'Poor little Harry!'

The village street looked very pleasant as Harry strolled along on her way to the village stores, the following afternoon. It was warm and sunny, and at that hour of the day, when the children had gone back to school and their mothers were still tidying up after dinner in their cosy thatched cottages, it was very quiet indeed. The late spring sunshine beat down on her neatly piled hair, turning it to an even brighter gold; she was wearing a sleeveless knitted dress, the same pale pink as the washed walls of the cottages, and she looked prettier than ever despite her dismal feelings. There was no one in Mr Smallbone's shop; only Mr Smallbone himself, standing behind his polished counter. It was dim inside and smelled pleasantly of biscuits and coffee and, more faintly, of cheese. She put her basket down on the counter in front of him and he took off his glasses and beamed at her and said in his creaky old voice,

'Good afternoon, Miss Harriet. Home again, I see.'

He always said that, ever since she had gone to hospital to start her training, and as always, she smiled and said, 'Yes, Mr Smallbone. Days off again. I've brought Mother's order.' She waited while he went through the small ritual of writing the name and address in his order book in a large crabby hand. This done, he put the pencil down, reached under the counter and brought out a tin of chocolate biscuits and proffered them with an air of long custom—which indeed it was; she could remember Mr Smallbone's biscuits back through the years. She

took one now and started to nibble at it the while
she started on her list. They were debating
the type of bacon she should purchase when
she heard the shop door open behind her.
Mr Smallbone looked over her shoulder and
said, 'Good afternoon, sir,' and Friso's voice
answered him.

Harriet had no breath in her body and her heart
was thumping madly. She looked unseeingly at
the side of bacon Mr Smallbone was holding up
for her inspection, then cautiously turned her
head and stared unbelievingly. She closed her
eyes and opened them again; Friso was still
there. Her heart had got into her throat, making
it hard for her to speak. She swallowed it back
and managed, 'Friso,' in a dieaway voice, and
then, 'It is you, isn't it?'

'In person, my dear girl. And how is Miss
Slocombe? Are you enjoying your new status as
Ward Sister?' He studied her carefully with a
faint smile. 'I can't say it's improved your looks.
Maybe it isn't your true vocation in life,
after all.'

She had been feeling pale, but this remark
brought a fine flush to her cheeks, and because
she felt uncertain she said rather crossly,

'If that's all you came to say, you can go
away again!'

She turned her back on him, although it cost
her an effort to do so, and said loudly to Mr

Smallbone, I'll take the small back, I think, cut on number seven.' And heard Friso say, just as though neither Mr Smallbone or the bacon had been there, 'No, it is by no means all I came to say, and I have no intention of going away.'

Mr Smallbone finished writing about the bacon and looked up, not at her but over her shoulder at the doctor. He said nothing, but his blue eyes twinkled as he took the list from her unresisting hand, laid it tidily in the order book, and came from behind his counter to cross the shop to the door, where he turned the 'open' sign to 'Closed', pulled down the old-fashioned linen blind and turned the key in the lock. With the faintest glimmer of a smile at them both, he walked back again, opened the lace-curtained door at the back of the shop and disappeared behind it. In the utter silence which followed, his voice could be heard—a faint dry murmur, followed by an unmistakable chuckle. Harriet still had her back to Friso, but when he said quietly, 'Turn round, Harriet,' she did so. After all, she couldn't stand for ever with her back to him. She did it reluctantly, though, holding her shopping basket in front of her like a shield. There was a loose strand of cane in the handle, and she began twisting it and untwisting it; it was something to do. She watched Friso, wondering what he would say, and was conscious of disappointment when he remarked casually,

'I've been to see your parents.'

She thought about this for a moment; there seemed no suitable answer, so she said 'Oh?' in a cool voice, which, despite her efforts, held a small tremor. She said 'Oh' again in a quite different voice, however, when he thundered, 'Leave that damn basket alone and attend to me, Harry!'

He was, she saw, quite exasperated and very tired. The sight of him so made her want to cry, but crying was something she had done a great deal of in the last two weeks, and she had no intention of starting again.

He smiled suddenly and tenderly and the tiredness vanished.

'Let's get one thing clear,' he said firmly. 'It's you I shall marry, my pretty.'

'But how can I be your pretty?' She had lost control of her voice and was appalled to hear it spiral into a near-wail.

'Ah, yes,' he interposed, 'I should have explained, but seeing you again has emptied my head of all good sense.' He walked towards her, coming so close that she was forced to tilt her head back to see his face. His great arm folded around her to crack her ribs with its strength.

'This first,' he said quietly, 'for I have no more patience.' He bent and kissed her mouth with a tender fierceness that blotted out the ache in her ribs. 'My dear darling,' he said presently,

'I've loved you since we first met—I fell in love with you five weeks ago when I saw you in Franeker, standing on the pavement staring at me with your great blue eyes and smiling.'

'Did you really?' asked Harriet with interest. 'You looked at me as though I were a lamp-post!' She was prevented from enlarging upon this nonsensical idea by the simple expedient of being kissed again—something which proved so satisfactory to them both that there was quite a pause before Friso said,

'I couldn't quite believe that I had found you at last.'

'But you drove away.'

His eyes were dancing, though he answered gravely enough.

'Against my inclination, my lovely girl—luckily common sense prevailed. You see I was pretty sure who you were; I knew that I should see you again—and soon. I could hardly leave Roswitha in the middle of Franeker while I. . .'

'Roswitha,' said Harriet rather sharply. 'The brunette—the beautiful brunette. . .'

'The *dominee's* daughter—occasionally I give her a lift in the car. She works in Alkmaar.'

'And the beautiful blonde—the one at Sieske's party?'

'The daughter of an old friend—I had to bring someone, you know.' He was laughing at her until she said, 'Oh, Friso, dear! Please explain.

Taeike told me you were going to be married.'
She looked at him, appalled at her muddled
thoughts which somehow had to be voiced. She
had her mouth open to speak when he put a
gentle finger on her lips.

'No, listen, my dear love, listen to me. You
shall scold me later if you wish. I promise that
I will be meek.'

She was between laughter and tears. 'Friso,
you're never meek!'

'Am I not? In that case, I daresay we shall
quarrel a great deal when we are married—that
is, if we can find the time, for I shall have my
patients and you will have the children.'

She felt his arms tighten and sighed deeply,
a sigh of pure content. 'Shall we go sailing in
your *botter*?' she asked. 'You said once that it
was very suitable for children.'

He said, his deep voice full of laughter, 'I can
see that, what with quarrelling and sailing and
bringing up children, we are going to lead a very
busy life; although there will be time for other
things—such as this.' He bent his head again,
and for the moment at any rate, Harriet forgot
all about the *botter*. Rendered breathless, she
nevertheless managed to repeat, 'Please explain,
Friso. I've been so unhappy.'

'It was Taeike—and I blame myself; for it
should never have happened. You see, dearest,
I have known her since she was a toddler and

to me she was—is still a child. But she's fourteen, you know, and has her mind full of dreams and fancies—' he paused. 'She saw that we loved each other and she tried to stop us. When you were in Amsterdam she came to see me— she told me that you were going to marry someone in England, she showed me a snapshot of you both. I had no reason to disbelieve her. It could have been true, for sometimes you behaved as though you couldn't stand the sight of me, and I had let you see that I cared, but I had to be sure that you felt the same way.' He stopped and kissed the top of her head in a contemplative manner. 'I learned the whole a few days after you left; she told me then that she had told you a similar story, but she likes you very much, Harry, and she couldn't bear to make us unhappy any longer.' He chuckled. 'It was a snapshot of your brother, by the way.'

'Poor Taeike,' said Harriet, in a voice comfortably muffled in his shoulder.

'She'll get over it, darling—already has, for I told her that when she would be old enough to marry me I should be as old as her father. I fancy I shall be looked upon in the light of an uncle in future.'

Harriet reached up and clasped her arms around his neck. 'None of it matters, does it?' she said. They smiled at each other and then drew apart; the faint squeak of the door sounded almost apologetic.

Mr Smallbone peered at them with a conspiratorial air. 'The afternoon trade,' he murmured.

Friso loosed Harriet. 'Of course,' he said, and went and changed the sign round again, pulled up the blind and opened the door on to a small group of puzzled and slightly indignant housewives. He smiled at them with charm, so that they smiled back, mollified, their ill-feelings forgotten. He ushered them into the shop and went back to stand by Harriet. He looked across the counter at Mr Smallbone, and said loudly enough for everyone there to hear him.

'Thank you for your kindness, Mr Smallbone. Perhaps we can repay it in some small part by inviting you to our wedding—tomorrow morning at eleven. In the church, of course.'

He took Harriet by the arm and led her out of the shop amidst a sudden outbreak of excited talk. Outside in the road she stopped and peeped up at him, and said almost timidly,

'Friso, dear Friso, you can't mean eleven o'clock tomorrow.' Her voice wavered. 'The hospital—my work—Mother and Father—no clothes. . .' her voice faltered and rose to a squeak. 'The licence!'

He tucked her arm rather more firmly into his. 'I don't think I've forgotten anything,' he said with calm. 'My dear love, why do you suppose it took me so long to come to you?'

They started to walk down the road, between the cottages. Harriet felt her hand taken and held in Friso's own. It all seemed impossible, but if he said that everything had been arranged... they would be together for always. As though he had read her thoughts, she heard him say, 'Remember our Friesian oath, darling? I told you then that loving is for ever.'

MILLS & BOON

BETTY NEELS

COLLECTOR'S EDITION

If you have missed any of the previously published
titles in the Betty Neels Collector's Edition our
Customer Care department will be happy to advise
you of titles currently in stock. Alternatively send in a
large stamped addressed envelope and we will be
pleased to provide you with full details by post.
Please send your SAE to:

Betty Neels Collector's Edition
Customer Care Department
Eton House
18-24 Paradise Road
Richmond
Surrey TW9 1SR

Customer Care Direct Line - 0181 288 2888

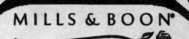

MILLS & BOON®

*B*etty Neels is a unique and much loved author and, as you will know, she often uses medical settings.

*I*f you enjoy stories with a medical flavour, featuring doctors and nurses battling to save lives and find lasting love—and peopled with characters as heartwarming as those created by Betty Neels, then look out for the Mills & Boon series,

Medical Romance™

which features four new stories each month.